CU00404550

SPRING IN MY STEP

An erotic novella

Sallyanne Rogers

Published by Xcite Books Ltd – 2014

ISBN 9781783756605

Copyright © Sallyanne Rogers 2014

The right of Sallyanne Rogers to be identified as the author of this work has been asserted by her in accordance with the Copyright, Designs and Patents Act 1988.

The story contained within this book is a work of fiction. Names and characters are the product of the author's imagination and any resemblance to actual persons, living or dead, is entirely coincidental.

All rights reserved. No part of this book may be copied, or transmitted in any form or by any means, electronic, electrostatic, magnetic tape, mechanical, photocopying, recording or otherwise, without the written permission of the publishers: Xcite Books, Suite 11769, 2nd Floor, 145-157 St John Street, London EC1V 4PY

To Esps, Smiffs and most of all Alberts

Chapter One

If we'd been honest with each other from the start, would it still have turned out the same way? I suppose it might have been better, but then again, it could have been a whole lot worse. Some people make a big deal out of total honesty, but if everyone always told the brutal truth, straight up, most of us would hardly get laid at all. That night in the Harlequin Bar, I think both our minds were running along an identical track: time enough to mention the you-know-what when you've decided whether you want to take it any further, thanks. We were drunk, we were horny, and we'd both decided, ironically enough, that the other one looked good on the dance floor.

It was a night when I knew I was looking good, anyway. I'd re-dyed my short, spiky hair a darker shade of pink about a week ago, and found a truly amazing pair of neon-pink trousers that were actually long enough for five-foot-ten me in the Cancer Research shop that afternoon. It was my former flatmate Joanna's 29th birthday, and she had decided to round up all the old gang, along with some of her other friends, for a night in the Harlequin, which was a club I hadn't been for about three years, so it was great to find that it hadn't changed at all. It was still two floors of dark, dirty, slightly weird-smelling mayhem; still home to a high percentage of tattooed, pierced, freaky but interesting people.

Just as we'd always done back in the days when six of us lived in two adjoining flats close to Shoreditch station, we spent the first couple of hours in the upstairs bar, piled round the big table at the back, catching up on what we'd all been doing since the last time we'd met up. It was only once the wine and gin had really started flowing that we decided to head downstairs and shake our stuff to whatever mix of retro-punk-indie-metal was going on down there. At the end of the night, probably, we would hit the fried chicken shop and try to fend off any hangovers with bucketloads of carbs and grease. Unless anyone got a better offer, of course.

I wasn't really thinking about better offers when we started dancing. I hadn't had any I felt like taking up for several months, not since Phil and I agreed, amicably enough, that we were tired of a relationship that didn't seem to be going anywhere. As for my mates, Joanna had her long-term partner, Miles, with her; some of the other girls seemed to have dates with them, some didn't, but no one seemed to mind either way.

I spotted Robbie, though I didn't know what his name was then, about halfway through a frenzied thrashabout we were all having to The Libertines. He was difficult to miss, being well over six feet tall, with messy blonde hair and a sleeveless white T-shirt. Niiiiice, I thought, and danced my way into his line of sight. He clocked me, or I think he did, but all the bodies bouncing off bodies stopped me getting any closer, so I carried on enjoying the music. Once I'd noticed him, though, I kept on noticing him, even as we all wandered on and off the dance floor, slipping in and out of shouted conversations and taking turns to fight our way to the bar. Because dancing is such a big thing for me, I do pay attention to how other people move and, just like anything else, some people can really do it, most are basically OK, and there are some you couldn't teach to hear the beat at gunpoint. This tall-fair-and-glorious was one of the ones who definitely knew what his feet were for. If I hadn't had quite so much cheap gin in my bloodstream at that point, I might have worked out just what it was about his moves that got to me, but I don't think I even considered it. Not then, anyway.

So there came a moment when we were elbow to elbow at the bar. I hadn't engineered it – much – but he looked down at me and grinned, and I got this glorious, shuddery rush all up and down my body, from my upper lip to my lower ones, if you know what I mean, and I said something like, 'Sorry, were you here first?'

'I don't mind coming second,' he said, and we both got the giggles at the sheer filthy cheesiness of that. We swapped names, then – Cath and Robbie – and chatted a bit. Do you come here often, no, not been for ages, are you local, it's my mate's birthday, I'm out with people from work, blah blah, good music here, yeah but bar staff straight out of *The Walking Dead*.

The last bit had always been true in the Harlequin, which seemed to pick employees for their above-average sulkiness and slow-moving incompetence. A good ten minutes later, neither of us was any nearer getting served, but we'd bonded some more over a mutual loathing of *The X Factor* and football – his workmates' preferred topics of conversation, by all accounts – and discovered that neither of us was a morning person. Then the Kaiser Chiefs came on and he put out a hand and asked me if I'd like to dance.

If watching him dance had attracted me initially, actually dancing with him was the thing that finished the job. It was as though we were reading each other's minds: even though we hardly touched each other at all, every move we made was in harmony. We stayed on the floor for another two tracks and then the DJ put on some awful doom-laden death metal thing, and we looked at each other and headed back toward the bar.

'Let me get you a drink,' he said. 'I got paid yesterday.'

I said yes, thanks, gin and tonic, and then excused myself and bolted off to the loo. I was so turned on I was almost scaring myself. My face felt hot, and I could feel how hard and erect my nipples were, and wanted to check they weren't poking too obviously through my bra and shirt.

Of course, when I got there, Joanna and Meg were propping up the sink and having a gossip, and both of them wanted to know how I was getting on.

'We saw you dancing with Eric the Viking, or whatever he's called,' Meg said with a grin. 'Does he know you're nearly famous?'

'Oh, do fuck off,' I said, but not nastily. 'I told you, no one's going to see the bloody thing, if it ever gets broadcast. It'll be on the Single White Insomniac channel at four in the morning, you wait.'

'And all over YouTube the next day,' Joanna said,

and I growled at her. They dropped the subject after that, but at least it had reduced my physical state to something more like normal, and neither my face nor my chest gave any indication that only a few moments ago I'd been seriously wondering if I was going to come just from standing next to him.

What Meg and Joanna had been teasing me about was a documentary I'd been roped into, which I'd been daft enough to tell them about earlier on. It's not that I've ever been ashamed of my hobby – I love it and I'm pretty good at it, and so are the rest of my teammates – it's just that I have heard every single joke on the subject a million times before, and I didn't feel inclined to have to listen to them again from somebody I was pretty keen to pull. Yes, Morris dancing suffers from a bit of an image problem, if you believe the mainstream press, but then so does pretty much everything that doesn't involve Z-list celebrities and shopping. I love dancing, I love performing in front of an audience, I have a soft spot for tradition – especially the kind of tradition that you can play around with – oh, and I like the drinking and general misbehaviour that's a massive part of the whole scene. I also liked being part of my own team, the Waterleigh Wenches, as we were more than a little bit controversial, according to some people.

Playing around with tradition? That was us: depending on who you asked, we were either a bunch of excitingly subversive modernisers or attention-seeking slappers who should be banned. I thought we were having fun and waking the audiences up a bit. Probably one of the reasons Jo and Meg switched pretty rapidly to telling me that Amanda, another of the gang, had pulled someone who was supposedly the drummer in a band was in an attempt to head me off before I started ranting on about Morris stuff again ...

I was a bit worried that I'd been in the ladies' long enough for Robbie to think I'd vanished on him, but he was leaning against one of the pillars at the end of the bar when I finally emerged, holding a drink in each hand and talking to a rather self-conscious looking bloke with short hair and too-clean jeans on, who I guessed to be one of the aforementioned workmates. Robbie spotted me and grinned, raising the glass that hopefully held my gin – it ought to, as the other one was a pint. He didn't introduce me to Clean Jeans, but then the workmate, or whoever he was, showed no interest in meeting me and took himself off the minute I got there.

So Robbie and I drank our drinks, and talked some more, and then we danced some more, and it was just as good as it had been earlier. The pace was a lot faster, and people were starting to bash into each other a bit more, but that was OK. One surge of what looked like veteran punks knocked me right into Robbie, but he just put one arm round me and pulled me against his long, lean body, and that was definitely OK. I could feel the heat of his hand between my shoulder blades and all my nerve ends were tingling. Robbie grinned, and then he kissed me. It wasn't tentative, but it wasn't too pushy either, and I kissed him back before breaking away with a grin of my own. We carried on dancing, then, but I found myself speculating silently about what he might look like naked, and once again, a steady pulse of arousal started up between my legs. I knew I wanted to have him, and was pretty sure he felt the same way: when we'd been briefly wrapped around each other, I'd been pressed up against something that indicated he was interested, put it that way.

The thing was, now I lived in South Waterleigh, which was a good way further west, I'd arranged to crash on Joanna and Miles's sofa that night rather than braving three different night buses to get me home. It wasn't that I thought either of them would object to me wanting to entertain a guest, it was more that, having slept on that sofa before, I knew just how uncomfortable and how bloody small it was. I wondered where Robbie lived, and who with, and it actually occurred to me to suggest sneaking into the ladies' for a quick one up against a cubicle wall, it being far too cold for getting up to anything in the dark alley round the back of the bar. I hadn't done anything like that for a couple of years, though I wouldn't say I'd never done it, but it had been a long, long time since anyone had turned me on the way he did.

It was getting late, now, and the Harlequin was starting to wind down a bit. There were even a few vacant seats around the half-dozen tables at the back of the room, and when Robbie saw me glance at them, he took my hand again and said, 'Let's sit down for a bit.'

'Good idea,' I replied, and we made for the nearest one. Neither of us said anything for a minute or two once we'd sat down, and then I offered to go to the bar, just as the loud chime of last orders sounded, and triggered a mini-stampede around us.

'Don't worry about it,' Robbie said. 'Not worth

it – the Undead'll never get half of this lot served before they close.' I shrugged, but agreed that he had a point. Looking around, I saw Joanna and Amanda, who was hand in hand with a short, bearded bloke I assumed was the drummer she'd pulled, in a huddle with most of the rest of the gang, and wondered if I ought to bring up the subject of how we were going to finish the night, or if he would say something first.

'There's plenty of booze back at mine,' Robbie said suddenly. 'Well, at my brother's flat, anyway. I'm staying there at the moment because my heating's fucked and he's in Australia for a month. Do you want to come back with me tonight?'

I almost laughed with sheer relief. 'Yeah, love to. Only reason I didn't ask you first was because I was going to be staying at my mates' tonight and it's a bit cramped. Just let me go and find them and tell them what's going on. Back in a minute.'

Of course, I had to endure a certain amount of piss-taking off Joanna and the others – Amanda having made a quick exit with her new friend – but in the end they wished me well and I went back to where Robbie was sitting, and said I was ready to go if he was. I felt quite glad that, having planned to stay with Jo, I had my toothbrush and a change of clothes in my rucksack. Though my intention was naturally to get to bed naked, with him to keep me warm, I was pleased that I'd packed the black satin nightshirt I got for Christmas rather than my tatty old pyjamas. It was the end of March, but fairly Arctic outside, which meant that Robbie had a coat in the cloakroom to queue for as well so I didn't have to feel awkward about keeping him waiting. It did occur to me that I might have let myself in for a murderous night bus journey anyway – and possibly an even worse one in the morning – if his brother's place turned out to be somewhere south of the river, but as we made our way out into the freezing night he said, 'It's not far, it's near Kings Cross.' Great, I thought, straight there on the night bus and straight home on the Piccadilly Line whenever I surfaced.

The bus was fairly crowded, so we had to stand, but neither of us minded much. I was very aware of the heat of his lovely body next to mine, and I liked the way he kept an arm lightly round me, one hand sliding up underneath my coat to rest on my hip with a little caressing movement from time to time. In a seat near the back, I spotted a couple snogging each other's face off and felt a mixture of envy and superiority. I thought there was something slightly adolescent about getting stuck in on a crowded bus, but at the same time, I was absolutely aching to take things further with Robbie.

We talked a bit, amused by the coincidence of both of us being away from home that night. He lived in Dalston, nearer the centre of town than me but not impossibly far away for any future meetings. If there were going to be any: I wasn't going to think that far ahead just yet.

Robbie's brother's place was not too far from the bus stop, on the top floor of one of those nice, partly gentrified Victorian terraces, and he made some crack about it being not much better than his own flat, just a bit tidier.

'What do you want to drink, then?' he said, once we were settled on the big, low sofa. 'He's got most things – gin, whisky, wine, lager. There was some bitter, but I nicked that last night, and it was fairly rubbish stuff anyway.' I asked for gin, and it turned out that the only thing to mix it with was cranberry juice, but it wasn't too horrible a combination. Robbie got himself a whisky and water, and put on a CD of something that wasn't all that familiar to me: Gothy, atmospheric stuff with a deep-voiced male singer. I quite liked it, though. The flat was gloriously warm, as well, which might have made me sleepy if I hadn't been feeling so incredibly aroused. It seemed like every nerve ending I possessed was throbbing with anticipation, yet at the same time I wanted to draw out every second, stay right there in the moment.

Robbie put his drink on the low wooden table and lay back on the sofa, pressing his leg against mine.

'Do you want to come here?' he said, and there were several ways I could have taken that remark. As it was, I put my own drink down and leant languidly over him, very slowly bringing my body closer to his. I kissed him, a bit carefully at first, but he brought a hand up to cup the back of my head, his fingers gently caressing the very short, spiky hairs at the back of my neck. We both opened our mouths a little as our lips met, and our tongues made contact. He put his other arm round me, pulling me down to lie on top of him, and I could feel how hard he was. I had one leg draped over his, the other drawn up on the sofa so my still-clothed crotch was resting against his covered shaft. I began to wriggle my hips, slowly and rhythmically, rubbing myself against him and he held me tighter, beginning to push upward, and all the time kissing me, the kisses getting deeper and more intense. The seam of my tight pink trousers pressed against my swollen clit through my sheer little knickers, and I was aware of getting wetter and wetter from the friction.

Robbie took hold of my hips, clutching me against him, and whispered, 'Do you want to come? Do you want to do it like this the first time? I'm pretty close myself.'

'I want to see you,' I said, even though I knew that I was nearly at the point where I wouldn't be able to hold myself back. 'I want to touch you.'

'Yeah, touching, that sounds good,' he said.

I raised myself up enough for us to be able to undo each other's pants and stick our hands inside, but it was a little bit clumsy and awkward, so I said, 'Let's get undressed, it'll make life easier.' Pausing for a minute helped me get a bit more control over myself, as well. I wasn't entirely sorry; I wanted to savour it, not just let loose in a clumsy tangle on the sofa and fall asleep.

'Let's get into the bedroom, as well. There's more room on the bed.'

I told him that was his best idea yet and, hand in hand, we hurried across the hall to what he assured me was the spare bedroom rather than his brother's lair.

The fact that we'd left our shoes in the hall meant it wasn't too difficult to yank off socks with trousers, but we did both just chuck everything on the floor as we stripped, being far more intent on each other's bodies than on tidiness. The one thing he did do was grab a pack of condoms out of his jeans pocket and stick them on the bedside table, which saved me having to run back into the front room and scrabble desperately in my bag to see if I had any.

Naked, Robbie was every bit as gorgeous as I'd expected: smooth-chested, his skin very slightly olive-toned all over. The intensity of mutual lust had eased up a little after the clothes-removing pause in the action, so we were able to take our time. I lay beside him, propping myself up on my elbow, and kissed his neck and then his nipples, feeling them stiffen against my lips and tongue. He stroked my shoulders and then the upper slopes of my tits and I wanted him to suck them, but when he started brushing his thumbs very lightly round and round each nipple, again and again, I forgot about sucking and moaned; I couldn't help it.

Clenching the muscles in my arse and my quim, I could feel how swollen and wet my labia had become, and wondered whether I was actually dripping with excitement. A similar idea seemed to have occurred to Robbie, because he stroked his way over the curve of my hip, down across my thigh, and then put his hand between my legs and started to explore me with his fingers. I shuddered with pleasure and parted my thighs as much as I could.

'Oh, you're lovely,' he muttered. 'Lovely and warm and wet. You're wet for me, aren't you, love?' He had two fingers inside me now, working them in and out. His cock was jutting upward, rigid and ready, the foreskin right back and the head of it glistening with moisture. I wrapped my hand round it and gently squeezed, enjoying the heat and strength and hardness of it.

'Can I fuck you?' he said. 'Can I just fuck you, Cath? You're amazing, you drive me crazy.'

My mouth had gone dry and I couldn't speak, so I reached over for the condoms, letting my boobs brush against his face as I did so, and he kissed them, lightly and teasingly. It was a challenge to get the little foil packet out of the box and open it while he was fingering and teasing my pussy, and I had to clench my teeth a couple of times in order not to just collapse onto my back and give in to the orgasm I knew was getting closer by the second. He took his hand away while I rolled the tight, slippery rubber over his hot, engorged shaft, and lay there sucking my juices from his fingers, something I found wickedly dirty and appealing. His total appreciation of me was a turn-on in itself, and I hoped I was making it clear to him that I was every bit as enthusiastic about his body and his cock and the prospect of having him inside me.

When the condom was in place, he took me by the shoulders and rolled me gently onto my back, before positioning himself between my thighs. He looked down at me and licked his lips, and said, 'Do you like it hard and fast? Or do you want it slow and easy?'

'Could you do it slow and easy?' I teased. 'If I asked you nicely?' He was gripping his thick, latex-sheathed prick and rubbing the head of it up and down my pussy lips.

'I can do anything,' he said. 'Well, just about anything. But maybe not for long, right now.'

I thought for a moment of teasing him a little longer, prolonging the anticipation, but I couldn't do it. I opened my legs even wider and said, 'Fuck me. Fuck me hard.'

He slid all the way inside me with the first thrust,

and raised himself up above me a little and said, 'OK, Cath, OK?'

It was almost like the very last second before you launch yourself down a waterslide or out of a plane, a delicious, shivery tension that was bringing me out in goosebumps. I tried to find a word and couldn't say one. I just let out a little gasping whimper of assent, and wrapped my arms around him, and he groaned and plunged himself into me. Away we went, hard and fast, pounding our bodies against one another, crying out and clutching each other, and I brought my legs up and wrapped them round him, pulling him even deeper in, feeling the friction and pressure of his pubic bone against my clit. Then I let go completely, the climax I'd been waiting for rushing over me like a tidal wave, unstoppable, making me dig my nails into his back and nearly bite my tongue trying not to scream. My pussy walls convulsed around his cock, gripping and squeezing him tight, and these spasms triggered a similar response from him. He bit my shoulder, then threw back his head and gave a couple of harsh, hoarse cries as he came in three or four powerful thrusts inside me.

We hugged for a while with him still inside me, then he got up and did the necessary condom disposal and bathroom visit. When he'd finished, it was my turn, and another moment of brief gladness that I had my overnight stuff like toothbrush and make-up removing wipes. The heating had gone off and the flat felt chilly, so I even dug out my black silk number and chucked it on before returning to the bed.

I had assumed, being fairly fuzzy with endorphins and drink as well as tiredness, that Robbie would be asleep when I got back, but he was awake enough to say, 'Don't just disappear tomorrow. We'll do it some more.'

Chapter Two

I hadn't rushed off rudely in the morning: I'd stayed for a cup of coffee, and that was some time after we'd woken up in a sticky sort of tangle, both of us horny enough for some touching and groping, and then some more. But it turned out that there were no more condoms, so I'd wanked him off over my tits and had him finger and caress me till I came pressed up tight against him and both of us kissing each other with lazy delight. Then I'd decided I ought to go home and so I'd showered and dressed and he'd made the coffee despite complaining that his brother's cappuccino maker was a bit poncy and difficult to use.

I'd told myself in the shower that it was probably best to leave with dignity and an air of mystery and all that. I wasn't really in the market for any kind of relationship even though he was the best shag I'd had in ages: I didn't want to go through all the business of fitting into each other's lives, telling him about the dancing and the documentary and all the rest of it. I had the impression he'd picked up on the way I was distancing myself, because he didn't ask to see me again. He did look at my bag when I picked it up and raise an eyebrow at the keyring hanging from the zip.

'CRB. What's that, a message to the world that you're safe?

I'd laughed, even though that was another joke I'd heard more than once. 'No, just my initials. Catherine Rose Bellingham. At your service and on my way.'

I went down the stairs cursing myself; spelling out my name like that could have sounded just a little bit desperate, and I definitely wasn't desperate.

I left the bit about my initials out of it when I was telling Susy and Leah, two of my teammates in the Waterleigh Wenches, all about the very sexy man I'd picked up on Friday. Tuesday night was practice night, as always, and the three of us were spending the latter half of it lurking in the corridor alongside the main hall. I'd actually forgotten the documentary crew were going to be there, getting some scenes of us working on our dances rather than just performing them, and so I hadn't bothered to wash my hair or put any make-up on, meaning I was happy to skulk in the background. Mercifully, after a minute or two, those of us who weren't being filmed had been told to get out of the way so we didn't talk or cough or bumble into shot at the wrong moment. Dawn, our team's founder and leader, was explaining the Addebury arm movements that were commonly known as "prick and balls", which had delighted the filmmakers, and the other two dancers who were at practice that night, Jayne and Belinda, were demonstrating them. Over and over and over again, until they had to be thoroughly sick of doing them. Well, Belinda and Jayne were the ones who had always been the keenest on the whole TV project, so let them do the hard work, I thought.

None of us actually hated the idea, once it had been properly put to us, or it wouldn't have been happening, but some people definitely had a bit more invested in it than others. Belinda, being our youngest member, seemed to be looking forward to being asked for her autograph or showing up in the pages of *Heat* magazine, though the rest of us were less convinced that this was what lay ahead. I thought, as I'd said to my old gang when we were in the Harlequin, that if the documentary got shown at all, it would be late at night on some cable channel no one watched and then it would never be heard of again.

It had taken Valerie, the director, a couple of long sessions in the pub with us to earn herself her golden Morris ticket for filming as it was. Susy had once been a researcher on a chat show and knew a fair bit about TV crews and the media in general, and how you could think you were going to get a sympathetic showing and end up being edited to look a total loser. And it would be stupid to forget how many people think of Morris dancing as something to laugh at, no matter how well it's done. But eventually, Valerie and her crew had convinced us that it was worth our while to be involved, and that it wouldn't take too much of our time.

Of course, we all knew that part of the reason Valerie wanted to film the Waterleigh Wenches in particular was because of our reputation – and our kit, the main cause of that reputation. Dawn and Mel, our fiddle player, had decided about five years ago that it would be fun to put together an all-female Morris side of good dancers with a flashy, trashy, blatantly attention-seeking kit. Initially, they'd kept quiet about what they were doing, then just launched themselves on the world – or at least West London – the following

May Day with a pub tour deliberately planned to cross the paths of a couple of other local sides who also toured the area on May 1st.

I hadn't been around then; I'd joined when they'd been going for about 18 months, after meeting Leah and Mel at Cecil Sharp House. I'd been feeling sorry for myself as Holly Bush Morris, the mixed team who I'd previously belonged to, had just fallen apart after one too many relationship tangles had led to people taking sides and ferocious rows all round. I'd decided to go along to that night's ceilidh, partly because there would be lots of other Morris dancers there, and I might be able to pick up some information or contacts and get myself a place in another team. Most people had heard something about the implosion of Holly Bush, including Mel and Leah. They were sympathetic, but they'd been more interested in the fact that here I was, a reasonably competent Cotswold dancer, in need of a new crew while they were in need of more members. When they then found out that I'd moved to South Waterleigh a couple of months previously, they were even more delighted to meet me.

'So what is it that you wear?' I'd asked, not having seen them perform. I didn't want to give up dancing, and I thought Mel and Leah were cool, but I drew the line at frilly pinnies or mob caps when it came to being seen out in public.

'Ah,' said Mel.

'Now that's where some people do bail out,' said Leah, and then they explained, properly, who they were and what they did. I thought they sounded like the perfect team for me, and said so, got an invitation to turn up to practice with them the following week, and never looked back. A lot of Morris sides' kit is rooted in 19th-century peasant outfits, and a lot of the stuff that isn't is rooted in 1970s folk-revival fashion, though there are exceptions. Holly Bush, for instance, all wore black jeans, red shirts, and ribboned waistcoats, which was the sort of thing that you could actually travel on public transport in, once you'd taken the waistcoat off, without getting stared at or insulted. The Waterleigh Wenches' kit, however, was going to need a holdall and a change of clothes for travel; that was clear. It was a kind of steampunk-influenced pirate wench costume: billowing-sleeved, low-cut blouse, wide, stretchy lace-up waistband and short wraparound skirt over thin leggings or dance tights, with bells strapped to low-heeled long boots. Apparently, they'd experimented with tricorn hats but found them far too likely to fall off or blow away, so now everyone wore fringed headscarves.

The look worked for me, despite the slagging the Wenches sometimes got from the more traditionally attired dancers; it was sexy and unsubtle but in a piss-taking sort of way. And it was more comfortable, at least to my mind, than a long skirt.

'So this chap you met looked like a decent dancer?' Leah asked, homing in straight away on what was, to her, the most important thing.

'Bloody hell, yeah,' I couldn't help exclaiming, and we all three giggled. 'Never shag a man with no sense of rhythm,' Susy recited, doing a moderately good impression of Mel. Our fiddle player was on the petite side, with cropped, mid-brown hair and a sweet, wide-eyed face that was completely deceptive;

she knew more obscene jokes than anyone I'd ever met and had a legendary track record when it came to pulling men, though she claimed to have quietened down a bit now she was in her 40s. Susy and Leah were both happily married but that didn't stop them taking a lively interest in what the single members of the team got up to. Obviously, I didn't go into too much juicy detail, because the possibility remained at the back of my mind that I might see Robbie again. It's all very well describing the finer points – or the rubbish ones, for that matter – of a man's technique to your mates if you know there's not the faintest chance of you introducing him to them, but if you think they might be facing one another across a pub table at some point, you really don't want someone like Mel going, 'Oh, are you the one who shouts "Respect the cock!" at the moment of orgasm?'

I did share that thought with them when Leah complained that I wasn't being forthcoming enough, and Susy said she remembered the first time her husband, Allan, met the rest of the team and got asked if he was a dancer or a shandy drinker, and he'd said he'd rather have a single malt, thanks.

It was probably just as well that Jayne stuck her head round the door at that point and asked us all to come back into the main hall.

'We're going to dance *Morning Star* all the way through, so we need everyone,' she said, brightly, then added in a lower tone, 'Three times, tops, and then off to the pub, OK? Dawn's being stern with the crew.' Dawn combined the roles of squire, founder, and foreman in the team, which meant she was completely the one in charge. She had a natural talent for it, she always said, she came from a long line of schoolteachers. We scuttled back inside and formed up a set of six with Dawn as Number One, while Valerie explained, a bit unnecessarily, that we should just do the dance and the cameraman would move round us while we did it.

'Tits and teeth,' Susy muttered under her breath to me as we listened to Mel playing the intro, and I tried not to snort with laughter. I wasn't the worst offender when it came to frowning or gazing at my shoes, but if I was preoccupied, I sometimes forgot to smile. "Tits and teeth" was what we always hissed at one another if we thought anyone was feeling grumpy or the audience looked less than appreciative.

I thought I was doing fine, but midway through the second half-hey of the chorus I experienced a sudden flashback to Robbie on the Harlequin's dance floor, swinging past me and round again in what was a lot like a perfect back-to-back, and promptly turned left instead of right.

'Other left, Cath,' Dawn yelled, and I recovered myself within a couple of steps but suspected that my fuck-up would be in the few seconds of footage they actually showed of this particular session.

At least the TV people declined our invitation to come to the pub that night, so we could have an enjoyable bitch about them once we were all settled round our usual table in the Three Horseshoes. Dawn started to look a bit frazzled after a while, and I wondered if she was regretting having agreed to the documentary. She yanked the clips from her white-blonde hair, letting it tumble over her face, and rubbed her eyes, and I felt a bit sorry for her. Most

Morris sides have a kind of executive committee of a Foreman to teach the dances: a Bag to take care of the bookings, a Squire to be in charge when the team's out and about, and a Treasurer to handle the money. Dawn basically ran the Wenches single-handed, with intermittent back-up from Mel, though tricky issues were always put to a team vote. It must have been tiring at times.

Just as I was working out a way of reassuring her that it was OK, we didn't really hate Valerie and co and we could see the point of taking part in the programme, Susy jumped in and said pretty much what I had meant to say anyway.

'And you never know, the exposure might be good for pulling,' Mel added, and everyone laughed, especially Belinda.

'Yeah,' she squeaked, sitting up straighter. 'If we make Morris look sexy and cool, I might not get dumped by the next fit bloke who finds out what I do on Tuesday nights.'

'Oh bloody hell, have you been dumped again?' Jayne said, a bit rudely, and Belinda stuck out her tongue.

'Well, it wasn't really because of the Morris. He's moving back to New Zealand in a couple of weeks so we agreed it was best to split up now,' she said.

Belinda was only 22, and one of those girls whose love life tends to be one disaster after another. She was pretty in a Gothic way: long black hair, a nose ring and a tongue stud, and sweet natured but a bit volatile: 'Up and down like a bride's nightie,' Mel had once said when Belinda was out of the room and the rest of us had conceded that she had a point. Bel was lovable, though, and one of our most enthusiastic members, which tended to endear her – and the rest of us, by association – to audiences in most places.

'We keep telling you,' Mel said, 'pick a Morris dancer to go out with. They get it. You never get any crap off a fellow dancer. I've heard most of the Kings' Men are single, for instance.'

'Oh *God*!' Dawn groaned, putting her head in her hands. 'Mel, stop teasing her, OK?'

Susy and Jayne were both laughing, and Leah was rolling her eyes. I reached over to pat Belinda on the arm.

'The Kings' Men are a bunch of knobs,' I said. 'They're one of those teams who think women shouldn't be allowed to dance at all.'

Belinda made a face. 'Oh, I hate teams like that. They make everyone think Morris dancers are all wankers.'

'They're all about a thousand years old anyway,' said Leah. 'And remember what Rachel always says about Morris men – it gets tricky when you have kids together and both want to dance on the same day.' Rachel was another Wench, whose sister and brother-in-law were also dancers – and parents as well, so she knew all about it.

'Oh, I don't know,' Mel piped up. 'Remember when we were out in Oxfordshire last summer and they were on the same tour as us? They've got a few new lads in now – some nice-looking ones and all, and they actually had the sense to put them all up for the same dance. Not bad at all, now I think about it.'

Susy and Leah joined in, and I racked my brains for a minute before remembering that the Oxfordshire trip was the one I'd had to miss due to a cousin having picked that day for her wedding. Certainly the last time I'd encountered the Kings' Men had been about two years ago and there had been no sign of good-looking younger men at that point; just an old fart whose belly was nearly shooting the buttons off his shirt, who'd spotted my Wenches kit while I was queuing in the beer tent and got right up in my face about teams who were a disgrace to the Morris. I was still a bit thankful for the arrival of Susy and her husband just as I was trying to decide whether the trouble I'd be in if I punched the git in his fat, beardy gob would be worth it for the sheer satisfaction.

A lot of Morris dancers did stick to dating other dancers; it couldn't help but make life easier if your other half understood your hobby. Some people hardly socialised at all outside the folk scene, but I quite liked to catch up with my other mates, such as Jo, from time to time, and after the disasters with Holly Bush, I had reservations about the idea of getting involved with a Morris man. For one thing, you'd end up with everyone knowing your business whether you liked it or not.

I wrinkled my nose and took another gulp of my pint, just as Susy said to Belinda, 'You ought to go out on the pull with Cath, then. She got lucky at the weekend, didn't you, Cath?'

I quietly cursed myself for having blabbed in the first place, but it was too late to do anything about it now, so I let them all whoop and applaud and gave them the same story Susy and Leah had already heard – tall, fair-haired, seriously hot, good fun but that was that.

'So, are you seeing him again?' Belinda asked.

'I don't know.' I said. 'Probably not. We didn't swap numbers. And I don't know where he lives or anything – like I said, it was his brother's flat we went back to.'

'You could go back there and ask, couldn't you? Or back to the club you met him in,' she said, and I had to bite my tongue not to snap that I wasn't desperate and wasn't going to act like it, thanks.

'Honestly, Belinda, it's not that big a deal,' I said. 'Anyway, I think he was just in the club that one night; he was with some workmates.'

Perhaps sensing that I was getting annoyed, Dawn turned the conversation to the fact that it was almost dancing season, and time for everyone to check their kit and see if anything needed repairing or replacing. Our blouses, skirts, and waist-cinchers were all made for us by Dawn's sister, who worked at a theatrical costumiers', and it was only fair to give her a reasonable bit of notice if anything major needed doing. I mentally ran through my own checklist – when I'd hung my stuff in the back of the wardrobe in September it had all been intact, though I had a feeling my dance tights were getting a bit on the saggy side. Still, that was just a matter of buying another pair: no need to trouble Debra with any sewing. Jayne said she'd have a close inspection of hers as there'd been a bit of a moth problem in her flat, and for some reason we all got into a bit of an argument about what moths would and wouldn't eat, with Mel swearing that they ate knickers and Leah equally insistent that they didn't and Mel must have particularly corrosive body fluids.

I usually got the bus back from practice with Susy and Jayne, who both lived on the same side of Waterleigh as me, and we chatted a bit on the way home about the various things we were going to do over the summer, and how many bookings we had. We'd recently confirmed with the Waterleigh Bridge Market that we'd go and dance at their May Bank Holiday event, which we were all rather looking forward to. They were making a special effort on the Saturday of the weekend, wanting to attract a decent crowd to the market, and apparently, they'd booked another Morris team, maybe two, and jugglers and a band and stuff. It was a kind of arts-and-crafts market, near the river, that had been around for ages and given a bit of a reboot in the autumn and was supposed to be really good, now. I'd kept meaning to go and have a browse anyway, but never seemed to get round to it. It's funny how you can live in a place for years but hardly ever actually take advantage of its attractions.

Once the other two had got off the bus, I spent the rest of the journey thinking about Robbie and wondering why I hadn't at least suggested meeting up again. It wasn't just the sex – though it had been pretty great. I had a feeling there was something a bit more, a definite connection. I started nibbling at my thumbnail, irritated with myself. I really didn't need the aggravation of making a relationship work. I had plenty of good friends and lots going on in my life. He was gorgeous, and I liked the fact that he could dance; he had an air of being totally at home in his own body, which appealed to me. But then maybe he hadn't got room in his life for a girlfriend either.

Maybe he was perfectly happy to leave things where we'd left them.

I wondered if he'd see the documentary when it was broadcast, and allowed myself to drift, for a minute or two, into a completely ridiculous daydream of him tracking me down through Valerie and her production company, and the two of us being reunited in a TV studio, with an audience full of baying drunks and toothless wonders shipped in from the nearest old folks' home, all gagging to watch us burst into tears or have a snog on camera. It was thoroughly silly, because I was one of the least important people in the programme: Valerie was mostly focusing on Dawn and Mel, and using the rest of us as background material. There was a certain amount of talking-head stuff, sure, but no one was being forced into doing it if she didn't want to. I knew they'd done a short interview with Belinda, as the youngest and the one who looked least like the average person's conception of a Morris dancer, and I was quite glad that she'd been there to do it so they hadn't been angling for me to fill the position. Dancing, in the middle of the team, being part of a group performance, I was fine doing that, but the idea of having to explain myself to the great British public wasn't high on my wish list. I just knew I'd either stammer or say something idiotic about feminism and freedom of movement, which was the sort of thing Dawn would do much better than me, and probably had already. I was going to get teased enough as it was, and if Robbie were to see the thing, I'd rather he just saw me dancing, and hopefully not fucking up. But of course he wouldn't see it. It was unlikely I'd ever see him again and I should just stop obsessing like a bunny-boiler, and write off the other night as a bit of enjoyable fun, and nothing else.

Luckily, someone else rang the bell as the bus passed the Asda superstore at the end of my road, or I'd probably have been sitting there with my mouth open and my thoughts in a spin all the way to the depot.

Back in my flat, I did a bit of a tidy-up while the bath was running, and even dusted my room and the sitting room, or at least had a go at them. It was certainly just as well that I hadn't met Robbie on a night when I'd have been expected to bring him back here: not only was my place its usual mess, but there were a couple of fairly big pictures of me and the other Wenches hanging on the wall, which would no doubt have led straight into the sort of conversation I'd been desperate to avoid. Maybe it was vain of me to have them on display, but they were genuinely good pictures. They'd been taken by Gerry, who was married to Rachel, and a Morris dancer himself as well as a photographer: he mainly did weddings and local newspaper stuff, but he liked to get a bit arty from time to time, and these pictures had been taken with special lenses and some or other camera trickery that looked really impressive.

I got into the bath and lay back for a good soak, trying to make all my whirling, repetitive thought patterns calm down. A hot bath, a mug of warm milk with cinnamon in it, and a good night's sleep: that was what I needed. Maybe I'd have some decently filthy dreams that night, and wake up in the morning with a better grip on myself, as well as more of a sense of perspective.

My life was going perfectly well; the documentary was going to be the television equivalent of "today's news, tomorrow's chip wrapping", and if I ever did bump into Robbie again, I'd handle it with perfect cool and dignity.

Nothing whatsoever needed worrying about. I was going to be absolutely fine.

Chapter Three

Despite sleeping perfectly well, I was crabby and out of sorts at work the next day. My job is providing IT support for the head office of Winston and Tarrant, a furniture supply company. In essence, I look after all the computer systems they use for tracking sales and deliveries and stock movements. Not the most thrilling or glamorous of careers, but it pays well enough to keep me going, and the rest of the IT department are OK to work with.

It was a dismal, chilly morning again: spring was slow in coming this year, so I was wearing a dark grey crewneck jumper and lighter grey trousers rather than one of the short-sleeved blouses I'd recently bought, when the sun had shone for more than half an hour and I'd started hoping for some nice warm weather. My workplace has a fairly relaxed dress code, which is one of the reasons I like working there: I'm not very keen on having to spend loads of money on suits and tights or keeping my hair looking "normal". Eyebrows might be raised if I turned up in a T-shirt bearing the name of some rock band or skin-tight denim shorts or something, but I generally get away with stuff that's plain and simple, and also practical enough for crawling around under people's desks, messing about with cables.

I'd told a few colleagues about the documentary; most of them knew I was a Morris dancer and didn't particularly care as they had their own hobbies, some of which were much more interesting, if that's the word, than mine. Peter, our section head, was a poker genius and had been on TV himself once or twice after winning some major tournament, and a couple of the in-house software experts were heavily into Warhammer. We all had an unspoken agreement not to piss-take, which generally worked well enough.

That morning, though, the bus had been held up and didn't arrive until ten minutes after it should have done, which made me three minutes late for my official start time. Mike greeted me almost instantly with a crack about my future awesome fame and not being able to get out of bed once I became a megastar. Mike has the next desk to me and is a bit overeager. He also has a tendency not to pick up, at all, on the fact that he's being annoying, and it was a real effort not to bark at him. Luckily, Peter was nearby and perhaps detected the look on my face, because he instantly steered Mike away and sent him off to the HR department to find out if they knew who had done something horrible to one of the printers the previous day.

Wednesday's a day we quite often go to the pub at lunchtime, but I wasn't feeling very sociable, so I contented myself with a quick run to the Tesco Metro across the road for a ham and cheese sandwich and a can of Coke. I ate at my desk while checking my email on my phone – using company computers for personal email or Pinterest or Twitter is frowned on, understandably. I decided to have a quick glance at

Facebook as well, thinking I might get through another level of Candy Crush Saga before the others came back.

I'm not actually a massive Facebook junkie. It's partly due to working in IT, which makes most people who do it a bit more paranoid about online security; less inclined to spill our guts somewhere any dubious bastard could read our embarrassing confessions and look at photographs of us gurning in nightclubs or dressed as giant chickens for some charity event. OK, it's useful for keeping up with people and, yeah, Candy Crush and Bejewelled Blitz are a bit addictive, but some of my friends seem to want to spend their whole lives on there, jabbering about every mouthful they eat, every TV programme they watch – and probably every dump they take as well.

There was a message waiting when I logged in, and I clicked on it without much interest – probably another mass heads-up from Jo about the next get-together she was planning.

But it wasn't. It was from Robbie. Shocked, I nearly knocked my Coke over.

Hiya,

There's only one of you by this name, and I can't tell anything from the picture so I hope you're the right one, i.e. the girl I met in the Harlequin. If you're not, delete and ignore, but if that's you, how about a drink some time?

And then he'd put his phone number.

I think I might actually have let out a bit of a squeal, so it was just as well I was on my own in the IT department. I blinked at the phone, scrolled up, scrolled down and refreshed the page, just in case I'd completely hallucinated it. For once, I was almost sorry I'd used a randomly scanned cartoon picture of a dancing ostrich instead of a photograph of myself on my profile. Then I logged out, shoved my phone back in my bag, picked up my can of Coke and drained the lot, which meant I produced the most reverberating burp imaginable, just as Mike and Peter and the rest of the crew came barrelling back in. The amount of friendly abuse I got for that enabled me to pull myself together and actually settle down to my work for the rest of the afternoon, but I couldn't quite shake off the warm glow of anticipation and, to be honest about it, lust.

Sometimes, I like to tease myself with a bit of delayed gratification, so when I got home I got some homemade chili out of the freezer and stuck it in the microwave to defrost. I washed up my breakfast things, boiled some rice, heated up the chili in a pan, and ate my tea in front of the 24-hour news channel. I followed the chili with a raspberry yoghurt, and it was only after I'd finished that I made myself a mug of Earl Grey, sat down in front of my laptop, and logged back into Facebook to read Robbie's message again.

Of course I was going to ring him. It was fine to ring him. After all, he'd gone to so much effort to track me down that it would have been rude not to respond. I licked my lips and called up his profile, just to remind myself of all the other good reasons I should get in touch. And maybe just to make sure there weren't any massive red flags, just in case. He'd opted for a pic that was actually him, and I spent a few minutes eyeing it up. Someone had snapped him leaning back against what looked like a bar, with a pint in his hand. He was wearing an open-necked, rather flamboyant white shirt that looked good on him, and his hair was all messed up, a little darker than I remembered it, but maybe he wasn't above a sneaky bit of highlighting. I thought there was something a bit familiar about what I could see of the pub he was in, but then again, a lot of pubs look pretty similar. Other than displaying an actual picture of himself, he was reasonably security-smart: there was not much information on him available to anyone he hadn't accepted as a friend.

I could stick with delayed gratification and send him a message, of course – there was no little green dot by his name to indicate that he was online, so I'd have to wait till he logged on again. But that was probably pushing myself too far. I dug my phone out of my handbag and keyed in the number he'd given.

'Hello?'

He answered just as I was sure it was about to go to voicemail, and I wondered if he'd guessed it was me and was making me wait.

'Hello? Bloody phone had gone through the lining of my pocket again, are you there?'

'Hi,' I replied. 'I had a message from you on Facebook.'

This was another little test, of course – would he be off-puttingly eager, or would it be obvious that he'd messaged me when he was a bit pissed and horny and now couldn't remember which girl I was?

'Cath? That you? I did get the right one, then.'

That sounded about right to me, so I acknowledged myself, and asked him how he was doing. We chatted for a bit and then he suggested meeting up on Friday night.

'Do you know the Queen's Head near Euston? It's got decent beer and the food's all right as well. Oh, hang on, do you have any, er, food issues?' I blinked. That seemed a bit of a peculiar question. Was he going to make some sneery remark about vegetarians or women's supposed inability to be rational about mealtimes (because we're all obsessed with being thin and all that)?

'No,' I said, after a noticeable pause, and he seemed to realise that he'd annoyed me.

'Sorry, that must have sounded weird. It's just that my team – I mean, my mates ... Look, there's two vegetarians, a vegan, one with a nut allergy and one who's just the world's fussiest eater and a pain in the arse about it. So at least, if you do need special food, I'll know of somewhere we can go instead.'

Interesting. I perhaps should have picked him up on the mention of a team – I know he'd told me he hated football, but the last thing I wanted to do was get involved with someone who was obsessive about rugby or cricket or, God forbid, chess. But I thought his concern was actually rather sweet, and we agreed to meet in the Queen's Head at seven o' clock.

It had been a while since I'd needed to have a wardrobe flap on a Friday morning. I'd got to the stage with Phil of not being particularly bothered to dress up for a date unless we were going somewhere special, which usually only happened on a Saturday anyway. I didn't want to look too boring when I met Robbie, but I didn't want to look like I was trying too hard either. Mind you, I didn't want to wear anything that would have the whole of Winston and Tarrant asking nosy questions about where I was off to, and if I'd found myself a man yet, and all the rest of it. In the end, I settled on black trousers, because you can't really go wrong in them, and a lightweight green jumper with a pattern of leaves and flowers in a darker green on it. I wore my good black boots, the ones I usually keep for clubbing or parties, on the grounds that no one at work would look at my feet. I did consider my underwear, as well, and wore the lacy, pearl-grey bra and matching knickers that I'd treated myself to with my Christmas bonus the year before. I realised, as I was leaving my flat, that I didn't actually know what Robbie did for a living – was he going to turn up in a suit, or bike leathers, or paint-splattered jeans and a ripped sweatshirt? I'd once gone right off someone who turned up for our second date in awful old-man polyester trousers and a peach-coloured shirt that needed a wash.

Robbie and I arrived at the main door of the Queen's Head simultaneously, which made us both laugh. He had on black jeans and the dark blue coat he'd been wearing the night we met, over a red shirt, and looked every bit as fit as I remembered.

'Perfect timing; I like that in a woman,' he said, and kissed me. It was just a light, social kiss on the cheek, but it still carried enough of a charge to make my nerves sizzle with excitement.

I told myself silently to calm down as we made our way to the bar: I wasn't desperate and I wasn't daft. If he showed himself up as an arsehole tonight, I was walking away, no matter how much my libido was going into overdrive.

For a Friday night, the pub was relatively quiet.

The Wenches had danced there the summer before last, and it was pretty much the way I remembered it: one of those solid, independent Victorian pubs that you find from time to time down little back streets and side streets in Central London that most people never get around to discovering. Well, until some bastard at the *Evening Standard* or *Metro* blunders in and writes about the place and it promptly gets rammed every night. Robbie asked me what I wanted to drink and I asked for a pint of Doom Bar, thinking I might as well start as I meant to go on. Some men, I had found, still got a bit peculiar about women not just drinking pints but actually taking an interest in real ale, but Robbie just nodded and said he was going to have the same.

We got a table near the fireplace, which was full of logs but not lit as the evening was reasonably warm, and for a few minutes, we did the slightly awkward first-date kind of conversation. He'd had his heating fixed, he said, and was now back in his own flat in Dalston. It turned out he was a graphic designer and worked at a small-scale print business in Hackney, and liked it. I told him a bit about Winston and Tarrant, but didn't go into much detail – there's only so much interest you can expect someone to take in the joys of debugging software, or the annoying personal habits of a set of workmates they don't know and aren't likely to meet.

Because it's generally not part of a Morris evening tour to sit down to a meal, I hadn't tried the food in the Queen's Head when I'd been there with the Wenches, though I had noticed at the time that what other pub customers were eating looked quite nice.

When we were going over the menu, I said that it all sounded nice, and that I'd been here before but not for a meal. Robbie said he had, as well, and told me about going to a pub in Essex that had a board offering Traditional English Pub Fayre: chicken tikka masala, lasagne, or fully loaded hot dogs. Tonight's choices included Thai green curry with jasmine rice and assorted stone-baked pizzas, but then this place wasn't making any bizarre statements about national identity. We settled on steaks and chips and, in another of those moments of synchronicity that are such a turn-on when you first get to know someone, discovered that we both liked our steak so rare it was still mooing.

I was turned on, all right. I felt hyper-aware of everything: the feel of my lacy underwear against my skin, the music playing in the background – some sort of slow jazz that I couldn't identify but rather liked – the mingled scents of food as the bar staff carried plates to tables, the fine, golden-brown hairs on Robbie's forearms …

I was enjoying myself, more than I had done in ages. The food was excellent too: the steak perfectly cooked, the salad leaves very fresh and the chips thin but not soggy. I've heard people say when they're out with someone they fancy the pants off they can't eat, but that's not something I've ever experienced. It was all going really, really well until we'd finished dinner and were on our third pint apiece.

We'd found plenty to talk about: favourite films, places we'd lived, assorted weird incidents on night bus journeys and how it was inherently wrong that Creme Eggs appeared in the shops the day after

Boxing Day but at the same time the rotten things were so delicious it was hard to object too strongly. Then we got on to the sort of things we liked to do in our spare time, and I was feeling relaxed enough and confident enough to say, without really stopping to think about it, 'Well, I'm a Morris dancer. My side's going to be on the telly in a few months' time; they're making a documentary about us. We're called the Waterleigh Wenches, and …'

'You're a … Bloody hell,' Robbie said, and I felt my mood of lazily relaxed anticipation drain away.

'Do you have a problem with that?' I hoped I didn't sound too belligerent. I didn't want to sound defensive either, but the look on his face wasn't one I much liked. I'd been prepared for polite interest or maybe a joke of some kind, but Robbie looked nearly as appalled as if I'd told him I strangled puppies or voted UKIP.

'No. No, of course I don't, why would I?' he said, and shook his head. 'It was just … you don't look like a Morris dancer.' He smiled, and it only seemed a little bit forced. 'You don't have a big enough beard. Or a beer belly.'

I made myself take a deep breath and smile back. 'You say the sweetest things,' I managed to reply. 'Took me ages to shave before I came out. I'm still working on the beer belly.' A part of me wanted to find the pictures of the Wenches I still had on my phone and see how many jokes he felt like cracking then. I considered telling him that the documentary crew had picked us as a perfect example of 21st century British culture, that we'd had a write-up on one of the bigger what-to-do-in-London websites for our "joyfully subversive reinventing of tradition", and that we'd been offered £1,250 to do a 20-minute spot at someone's birthday party last November, but in the end, I simply changed the subject instead. I wasn't so hideously offended that I was going to flounce out – I still had half my drink left, for one thing – but I wasn't having fun any more. I couldn't get over the look of horror that had crossed his face, and I was pretty sure that he'd come to the same conclusion as I had: there wouldn't be another date after this, and we weren't going to be deciding between his place or mine at the end of the evening.

We did carry on talking for another half hour or so, but it was definitely a case of making an effort to be nice, and when I looked at my watch and saw it was 10.45, I thought it was reasonable to say that I'd probably better be off home.

Robbie sighed, and said, 'Fair enough. I'll walk you to the Tube – do you want Euston or Kings Cross?'

'Euston is fine,' I said, and we made our way there in near silence. Strangely enough, it was quite a friendly silence, and when we stopped to cross a road, he took my hand and I let him. Once again, I felt that prickle and shiver of arousal at his touch, but I told myself to ignore it.

We reached the main station forecourt, and he said that he was going to get a bus. I said that was fine and thanks for dinner and a few other polite things, and he looked me up and down and then just reached out, put his hand behind my head, and pulled me close enough to kiss me on the mouth. I nearly melted on the spot; it was every bit as good as the very first one had been the previous Friday, on the packed dance floor at the

Harlequin. His lips were firm against mine, and there was just that slight, delicious additional pressure which made it clear that the kiss could get deeper and more serious if I wanted it to.

I did want to, I really did. I wanted to wrap myself around him and grind against his cock, dry-hump him in the middle of the station and then drag him back to South Waterleigh with me and fuck his brains out. But that was a bad idea. It would just be ignoring the fact that he had some kind of issue with something that was very important to me, and going to bed with him now would be like putting a nice new rug over a sodding great hole in the floor. I pulled myself away and said, 'Goodnight. Safe journey home.'

He let me go and then leant back in to kiss me once again, on the tip of my nose.

'I'll be in touch,' he said, and I nodded and walked away.

On the Tube, having changed to the Piccadilly Line at Green Park, I got my iPod out of my pocket and stuck the mini headphones in my ears. I always have it on shuffle just because I like hearing what it will come up with next, but I wasn't best thrilled to have it bombard me with one of the songs that was on my "great big stompy tantrums" playlist – *Inside Out* by Eve 6. I suppose it could have been worse than a bit of late-90s American college rock or whatever it was known as at the time, but iPods are not actually endowed with consciousness and don't have the ability to fill your ears with clichéd rubbish like *I Will Survive* when you would never have loaded any such thing onto them in the first place. Eve 6 was followed by Rage Against The Machine, which made me feel a bit better, and I was almost laughing at myself by the time I made it to South Waterleigh station. Robbie was good-looking and great in bed, but the two of us probably weren't compatible; it was as simple as that. Now that summer was nearly here and dancing season just about to get underway, there would be plenty of opportunities to meet and cop off with all sorts of blokes who weren't traumatised by the very thought of Morris dancing, if I found myself wanting a bloke at all. Which I didn't, really. I was a lot better off on my own, having a laugh with my mates, doing my job, lying on the floor in front of the telly watching *World War Z* on DVD, doing my Wenches thing in front of an appreciative crowd, and all the rest of it.

I wondered if Robbie had got home yet or not. I wondered what his place was like – was he tidier than me? Or a total slob with a sink full of dirty plates and cups, and spiders having abseiling contests from the light fittings? Once I was indoors, I stripped off my clothes and chucked them at the laundry basket without checking to see if they all went in. Then I stepped into the shower and spent a long time blasting myself with warm water, soothing my body and resisting the temptation to lean back against the tiled wall, get hold of the shower head, and see if the trick I'd read about so many times actually did work better than the average vibrator.

The last thing he'd said to me had been "I'll be in touch". It had probably been a polite way of ending a date that had taken a sudden swerve into no-thank-you territory, but then again, maybe he would get over his little freak-out and decide that I was worth bothering with after all. Maybe I'd misjudged him, or myself.

Catherine Rose Bellingham, you're like a human fucking seesaw, I told myself furiously, and then I got into bed, pulled the covers up over my head till I was totally buried in them, and closed my eyes. I had the feeling my dreams that night would be deliciously filthy or a load of absolute bollocks. Quite probably, they would end up being both.

Chapter Four

By Tuesday evening, when the time came to head off for practice, I was pretty much myself again. I'd given my flat a total spring clean and watched all the George Romero zombie films pretty much back to back on Saturday night, then spent Sunday slobbing in my pyjamas. I'd announced aloud to my kitchen cupboards on Monday morning that I was officially over the whole thing. After all, one shag, however good it might have been, and one date didn't amount to much.

Dawn had let us all know via the group email that Valerie and her crew were meeting us in the pub afterwards; they planned to show us some stuff they had of other teams so we could "see how it was all shaping up" and then do some on-camera interviews. She'd made it clear that there was no pressure on any individual member to participate, but we might be asked questions as a group, so it would be a good idea to make sure we had washed our hair and weren't wearing anything with food stains on it. I wasn't the only one who generally wore old, comfy, scruffy clothing for practice, but I suspected Dawn was thinking of the state I'd looked the previous week. Whatever, it couldn't hurt to make a bit of an effort, so that evening I had put on a relatively respectable pair of chocolate-brown yoga pants and my team promo T-shirt, which was red with a line drawing of a generic woman in a generic version of our kit on the front and "*Waterleigh Wenches – coming to get you!*" on the back in a rather curly-wurly font. I also put on a bit of mascara and a dark pink lip stain, just in case I ended up deciding I wanted to be interviewed after all. OK, it wasn't that likely, but I always liked to have the option of changing my mind about things.

It was a mild, dry evening so I got off the bus two stops earlier than usual and took the short cut past the allotments. I met Belinda just as I rounded the corner into Gafferton Road; she lived in Acton so was walking up from the Tube station. Like me, she was wearing her team T-shirt, and she'd done something fairly elaborate with her make-up.

'So, did you track down that fit man?' she asked, and I tried not to wince. There was no malice in her enquiry, just genuine interest: Belinda loved hearing about other people's romantic adventures.

'Well, yeah. I mean, no, he tracked me down,' I said, thinking I might as well tell her and get it over with. 'I saw him on Friday, but that was it. Turns out we're not really suited.'

She patted my arm. 'Oh dear, what went wrong?

'Like I said, not really suited. You know, he's nice enough but ...'

Belinda made a face. 'Well, if you don't want him, can I have him? If he's nice?'

She would have had no intention of upsetting me, and I was surprised at how much that harmless little suggestion stung me. I struggled for a moment and then said, 'He doesn't like Morris dancers. That's

48

why I'm not taking things any further.'

This was something Belinda understood all too well, so we got the rest of the way to the practice hall on a selection of her livelier dating encounters that had come to similar sticky ends.

With less than a month until May Day, we were all determined to make our practice time count, and Dawn really put us through it, especially as we were going to be finishing half an hour early in order to give Valerie enough time with us before the pub shut. Because we're a small team in terms of members – only eight dancers, where most sides have at least a dozen – everybody has to know every dance in every position so we can still perform if a couple of people can't make a particular date. We feature one or two traditional dances, but most of our repertoire is ones we've adapted or Mel and Dawn have constructed themselves. Out of the massive range of Cotswold styles, we generally stick to Addebury and Fieldtown, though we do play around with them a bit. Dawn was always very keen on challenging what someone had once described to her as the general public perception of Cotswold Morris – "well, there's one with sticks and one with hankies, isn't there?" What with that and an awareness we were never going to have that many spare bodies, a lot of the unique-to-us dances were for three or four people rather than the more common set of six. We'd been working on a new three-person dance since January, and Dawn was determined it would be ready for public performance in time for the Waterleigh Bridge booking, so we went through it about a dozen times that night.

We were all pretty hot and sweaty by the time we

locked up the practice hall and headed for the pub, and I think Dawn was wishing she'd told us all to bring a change of T-shirt or something, but we cooled down a bit on the walk down the High Street and when we got to the Horseshoes, we took turns bolting into the loo, to comb our hair or dab on a bit of concealer or pinch some of Katie's body spray if we'd forgotten our own.

It turned out that Valerie had booked the upstairs room at the pub, and she or one of her colleagues had ordered sandwiches and crisps and stuff, and they were buying all the drinks. I was sure I wasn't the only one suspecting that this might be due to them having a shock or two in store for us. Still, free food and drink was always going to be welcome, so we attacked the buffet and made polite conversation about the weather and suchlike for a few minutes. I didn't think I'd ever been upstairs at the Horseshoes, though I'd passed the little sign saying "Function Room" often enough on my way to and from the bar or the ladies', but it was as nice as the downstairs: white walls with the odd wooden beam but not too ostentatiously Ye Olde. Valerie let us chat and mill about for a while and then she drew our attention to the telly and DVD player she'd set up, and we settled ourselves down to watch what they'd shot so far.

At first, it seemed harmless enough: various very short clips of different teams dancing in different locations. There were a few bits of people practising: one lot looked vaguely familiar to me, and Mel said after a couple of seconds, 'Oh, those are the Hilltop HighSteppers,' and Leah said that we'd met them at Whitby last summer. Then there was a minute or two of us dancing our version of *Country Garden* on the South Bank, which had been filmed just after we agreed to take part in the documentary. I think we all found it a bit fascinating; it's not always easy to get an idea of what you actually look like in the middle of a dance, but I thought our performance was pretty good. I could see myself grinning away and was glad I'd been in a happy mood. If I made any mistakes, then the camera hadn't picked them up. There was a particularly nice shot of Belinda and me actually getting the stick-clashing right in the chorus, which made us smirk at one another – we were the two most likely to get it wrong if we were paired with one another in that dance.

Valerie paused the film at this point and asked if we were all OK for drinks. Mel, Leah, and Katie all said they'd have another pint, so I asked for another gin and tonic, and then Belinda wanted a Smirnoff Ice – a habit the rest of us had failed to break her of – and Valerie sent the smaller and more silent of her two cameramen off to the bar. I was pretty sure by now she was up to something, and wondered what on earth it was. She was one of those glossy-but-average women, probably in her late 30s, neither skinny nor fat, her features sort of unmemorable but attractive enough. Always well dressed, with her nails done and her hair like a shampoo advert. I watched her sitting on the edge of the table, chatting to Dawn and Rachel while we waited for the next round of drinks, and realised she was actually nervous. No, not nervous – I'd never seen her anything other than calmly in control before – but excited.

The way the documentary had been put up to us in

the beginning, after that dance-out at the South Bank, was as a "light-hearted look at Morris dancing in the 21st century", and we knew the Waterleigh Wenches were one of three or four different teams who would appear in it for more than just the opening montage. It occurred to me then, perhaps belatedly, that I had no idea about which other teams the crew were dealing with; if Mel or Dawn had been given any indication about it, they hadn't passed it on to the rest of us. Glancing discreetly from our musician to our glorious leader, I got the strong impression they either hadn't asked, or had tried and been fobbed off with vague generalisations. Dawn didn't look too pleased with the way things were going, though Mel didn't seem to care. Then Belinda passed me my fresh drink and I thanked her, and Katie leant across to complain that she had a pint of ESB instead of the Landlord she'd asked for, and had Leah got the wrong pint or what, and that occupied us all for a minute or two.

Valerie clapped her hands and we all turned to look at her. She'd stood up and strolled to the front of the room, and she was looking remarkably pleased with herself. I noted that the older cameraman was standing beside her, pointing his machine at the rest of us, and a quick look round the room showed me that the junior one was ready with a microphone on a stick.

'OK,' Valerie said. 'For the next bit, we're going to get some reaction shots. We did an interview with another team in January that we thought it would be good to get your take on, all of you.'

I reckoned I knew what was coming, and felt a weary sort of irritation. It wasn't going to be anything we hadn't heard before: Valerie and co would have tracked down some farty old Ring team and got them to huff and puff about how women shouldn't be allowed to dance Morris in public because it wasn't "traditional".

It was all absolute crap, of course: back in the days when Cecil Sharp, who's generally regarded as the founding figure of modern Morris, was at his most active, his contemporary, Mary Neal, was teaching the dances to her Esperance Girls Club. So women have every bit as much right to dance as men do, but you still get these silly sods who are afraid we'll look at them funny and make their cocks fall off.

Sure enough, when Valerie started the film again, there was a middle-aged man with a beard, clutching a tankard and looking like every viewer's stereotype of a Morris dancer, smirking into the camera and pushing his ribbon-trimmed hat back off his forehead. They'd filmed him from the waist up, but we could see that he was wearing a billowy white shirt, with crossed baldricks in red and gold, which matched his hat ribbons.

'Alfie Winters,' Mel said with a disdainful sniff. 'Should have known.'

'Who's he?' Belinda saved me having to ask, even though I was fairly sure I recognised the colours, and even found something familiar in his reddened, puffy, mean-eyed face.

'Kings' Men squire,' said Katie. 'Arsehole.'

I had it then: he was the one I'd nearly had a fight with when I was first in kit and dancing out. He didn't look like time had improved him much.

'Morris has always been a men's dance,' he was

saying to an off-camera Valerie. 'Women just can't do it properly. They haven't got the body mass for it, for one thing. Or at least what they have got isn't in the right place.'

If Valerie was expecting the Wenches to scream or faint or throw things, she was disappointed. We did hoot derisively at his opening remarks, and a couple of standard Morris Ring-piece jokes were made, but none of us started to foam at the mouth. For as long as I'd been dancing, the Morris Ring had always been the organisation that the rest of us regarded with an amused sort of tolerance: dinosaurs and silly old sods and mostly harmless. I knew from some of the stories I'd heard from Rachel and Susy, both of whom had parents who had danced in the 70s and 80s, that there had been times when it was all taken more seriously, with some heavy-duty feminist action required, but that these days pretty much everyone was a lot more live and let live about any Battle Of The Sexes stuff.

Evidently, no one had told Alfie Winters this, though. It sounded as though no one had informed him he was in the 21st century either. I supposed Valerie must have spent quite a while talking to him and just picked out the best bits to share with us, as he seemed to empty his tankard more than once as he really got going on his personal philosophy.

'It's like Angry Dudes on the Internet, Morris-style,' Mel said with contempt as we watched and listened to a progressively more unpleasant catalogue of what women were really good for. 'Valerie, do we have to watch any more of this? I think we've got the point. He's an arsehole. What more do you want?'

Valerie paused the film again. 'Well, there is just a

bit more – he talks about you specifically, and we really want to give you a right of reply here. Hang on, I'll find it.'

We groaned a bit and fidgeted, but were all too polite to get up and leave. The next clip she showed was Awful Alfie standing with a group of other men, all in Kings' Men kit, presumably on the same day but with no indication of whether this or his general rantings had been filmed first. The shot was wider, revealing that this was all happening outside a pub, and it was a cold day, judging by the hats and coats on various members of the public who were hanging around behind the Morris men.

'The Waterleigh Wenches?' He made a face I'd struggle to describe into the lens. 'Bloody disgrace. That's not Morris, what they do. And if they think showing their knickers will take people's minds off the fact they can't dance, what they've forgotten is it would help if they weren't all so bloody ugly.'

The camera crew got their desired reaction then: both Belinda and Katie shrieked with outrage, and as Valerie stopped the clip and turned expectantly in our direction, everyone spoke at once. Microphone Boy was skipping from foot to foot, trying to make sure he didn't miss anything, while Diane tried to respond with dignity and disdain and Mel offered some particularly colourful suggestions about the Kings' Men and their anatomical inadequacies. I heard it all, but I didn't say a word. I couldn't. I felt like someone had dumped a bucket of ice on my head, like I was a million miles away from the other Wenches, from the pub, from the whole planet.

There had been four or five other members of the

Kings' Men surrounding Alfie when he pronounced judgement on us and our dancing. They'd all been moving in and out of shot, maybe going to and from the bar or engaging in backchat with the crowd or other teammates or something, but I knew what I'd seen. One of them had been Robbie.

I wanted to view the footage again, but I wasn't going to ask, I just couldn't. I kept my hands under the table, clenching my fists, nails digging into my palms, running through it in my head, over and over. Robbie, standing behind that disgusting, obnoxious man, wearing the same team colours as him. The look of contempt on Robbie's face. Contempt for women Morris dancers? Or contempt for Alfie Winters? I wanted to think it was the latter, but then I would, wouldn't I?

I was aware that Valerie had enforced some sort of control on my teammates and was directing her crew to one after another of us, getting comments, asking questions, but I wasn't taking in anything anyone said. I was thinking about my night with Robbie, the two of us groping each other on the sofa, then naked together in the bed, skin against skin, hot and wet and burning with lust. 'You're amazing, you drive me crazy,' he'd said.

If I'd told him when we met that I was a Morris dancer, maybe none of it would have happened. Maybe we'd have laughed about it, maybe he'd have said, 'Oh the team I dance with hate women but I'm working on their attitude.' Or maybe he'd have said, 'Women shouldn't dance Morris,' and I'd have patted him on the head and just walked the fuck away. And none of it would have mattered.

I suddenly realised the cameraman was leaning over me, his mic-wielding sidekick right beside him and Valerie practically in my lap.

'Cath, how do you feel? We'd love a quote from you. You seem to have been very upset by that.'

I shook my head. There was a horrible temptation to give Valerie a magnificent bonus, the sort of storyline that people like her absolutely loved, and I got a flicker of awareness that she knew something of what was up and was craving details. I wondered for a moment what it would feel like to let loose, shout into their faces that I'd been mugged, conned, done over by one of the Kings' Men, but it was the same as standing on top of something high and wondering what it would be like to jump.

'They've all said it all,' I said, trying to sound as neutrally polite and uninteresting as I could. 'I've got a headache, I'm sorry.'

She didn't push me. For one thing, it was gone 11, and the landlord had already been up once wanting to know, in the nicest possible way, if we were going to be much longer. For another, Mel had shouted across that she had something else she wanted to say, and put it in the sort of colourful terms that we were used to but Valerie wasn't.

Jayne and Susy were still full of outrage even once we were on the bus back to South Waterleigh. I was rather hoping that they wouldn't notice how little I had to say for myself, and my luck was in for a while, but just before Jayne rang the bell, Susy turned to me and said, 'Are you all right? Is your headache still bad?' I'd almost forgotten my alleged headache by that point, but when I started to say that it was fine, thanks, I found myself welling up.

'It's pretty grim, to be honest,' I whispered, though I knew I was talking about Robbie rather than any physical pain. They were immediately concerned about me getting the rest of the way home by myself, but I managed to persuade them that I would be fine and not to worry, and kept a tight hold on what I knew was an oncoming fit of the weeps until I was actually walking down my own front path.

I was sniffling and dripping tears by the time I sat down at my computer, and rehearsing all kinds of blistering denunciations in my head. The fact that Robbie had sent me both a friend request and a message turned the sniffles into roaring sobs of rage.

Hey Cath, the message ran. *I want to see you again. There's something I ought to tell you. But I want to see you again anyway. How about Saturday?*

I turned away from the screen and allowed myself a good few minutes of real, head-in-hands crying. I was completely disgusted with myself. I'd been doing just fine as a single girl, quite happy with the idea that I might meet someone nice someday but equally happy that I might not. And then I'd picked Robbie up in a nightclub, had a good night – and morning – with him and walked happily away with only a tiny wistful wish to do it all over again. Going on a date with him had seemed OK as well until it all went wrong, and it would have been perfectly all right to leave it there without any drama, but now I'd found myself in what felt like some ridiculous Montague-Capulet star-crossed lovers bullshit situation, and here I was bawling away over something that really didn't matter at all in the long run.

'First World problem, First World fucking problem,' I growled, and snuffled, and went to find a bit of kitchen roll to blow my nose on. Once I'd done that, I rummaged in the kitchen cupboards until I found the miniature of sloe gin Susy had given me at Christmas, and drank it down in one before I went back to Facebook.

Fuck off! was the first post I typed, and deleted within seconds. It might be what I wanted to say, but it wouldn't exactly have the desired effect. Then I constructed a more measured response, all very carefully, diplomatically worded.

Dear Robbie.

I've found out the reason why you were so appalled that I'm one of the Waterleigh Wenches. I've seen the film of you in your Kings' Men kit hanging out with Alfie Winters. I'm amazed I actually got a shag out of you because anyone who hates women that much usually can't get it up. Don't even think about trying to get in touch with me again. Or I'll have you killed.

By the time I'd finished that one, I was laughing and crying at the same time. 'I've seen the funny side. I have, honest,' I kept saying, and rather wishing there was someone there to say it to. I tried hard to think about the moment when I'd be able to share the whole stupid thing with the rest of the team, but there was still a tight sort of pain in my chest. I deleted what I'd written, and went to make myself a cup of tea. It was nearly one in the morning, and I had to get up for work, so it was time I got a bit of a grip. I gritted my teeth really hard and wrote a third reply.

This isn't going to work for me. Have a nice life.

I made myself send it straight away, without any more hesitations: cool, polite, and assertive, it was the perfect "you're dumped" message that didn't give anything away.

I shut the PC down and sat in the armchair to finish my tea. I was sure Dawn and Mel and the rest of the team would have given plenty in the way of counter-argument to the ridiculous rubbish the Kings' Men were coming out with. I also told myself the TV crew were probably only using that footage of Alfie Winters in order to show up the type of useless, elderly, woman-hating, shit-for-brains dancers like him for what they actually were. I thought of all the festivals I'd been at with the Waterleigh Wenches, and all the fun we'd had, both in general and later at night when there were gatherings in various corners. Mel had a huge tent she'd got off eBay, and it was pretty common for the Wenches to pile into it at the end of the night for wine and ludicrous party games. I thought about playing some of those games with Robbie, and I went and stood under the shower with the setting on lukewarm, rather than cold.

What I wanted was to go to bed and sleep. I would get over Robbie within a matter of days, and summer was coming. It might even offer an opportunity to give the Kings' Men, especially Alfie, a little bit of a wake-up call.

Chapter Five

The rest of that week was pretty grim, but I thought I'd done a good enough job of acting like everything was normal. My workmates had never been the most observant bunch, though, so I probably didn't need to try as hard as I actually did. Still, it made me feel better to behave as though I was fine, which was a good reason for sticking to it.

On Friday evening, I was checking my emails at home, and found a reminder from Mel that the Spring into Action ceilidh was on Saturday night, and hadn't several of us said we were going to go along this year? I'd forgotten about it, but the idea seemed quite appealing.

Ceilidhs were usually fun wherever they were; I'd been to quite a few, both when I was dancing with Holly Bush and after they broke up. OK, sometimes there was a rubbish band or useless callers who either assumed that everyone knew the dances so well there was no need to explain them, or didn't know the damn things well enough themselves, but mostly you got people with loads of enthusiasm and knowledge up on the stage, so all that was needed from the dancers was stamina.

I'd slightly got out of the ceilidh habit when I'd been going out with Phil, as he hadn't been into the folk scene at all. Though he wasn't hostile about my involvement with the Wenches, he wasn't remotely enthusiastic about it either. I found myself thinking back to the six months we'd been dating while I was rummaging in the wardrobe on Saturday afternoon, trying to make up my mind what to wear. Phil had been a friend of a friend of Michael, one of the marketing blokes at Winston and Tarrant, and I'd met him at Michael's huge, shambolic birthday piss-up. My height, with broad shoulders and short brown hair, he wasn't stunningly good looking, but he had a nice smile and a daft sense of humour. It hadn't hurt that he didn't really have any connection with anyone I worked with: my lot got enough mileage out of me being a Morris dancer and I didn't fancy giving them any more opportunities to tease me about my personal life.

So Phil and I had started seeing one another, and it had been ... pleasant, I supposed. He worked in the accounts department of a car firm, and had an eye on promotion in a year or two, but didn't bore me with his five-point career plan. We went out for dinner once a week or so; sometimes we'd meet up with his friends in a pub or someone would have a party. I'd introduced him to my non-Morris friends, like Meg and Joanna, and I had taken him to Rachel's birthday party, and he hadn't disgraced me or himself. Sex with him had been pleasant too. He didn't have any peculiar fetishes, he wasn't a two-pump Percy and he never went in for excruciating "you love it, you bitch" fake-dirty talk. There was nothing wrong with Phil at all, but I didn't consider myself in love with him, and I didn't think he was in love with me either. A lot of women, apparently, would have considered me lucky to have a man like him.

Belinda was certainly bemused when I let the Wenches know I wasn't seeing Phil any more. She went on about it for quite a while in the Horseshoes that night, and when she was up at the bar getting crisps, Dawn leant over and said, '*Do* you want us to distract her? I know she doesn't mean any harm but ...'

'It's fine,' I said. 'It's not like I'm broken-hearted.' To be fair to Belinda, I was sure she wouldn't have carried on if I'd shown any sign of real distress; she wasn't that insensitive. She was simply struggling to comprehend why any girl would dump a man when there was no one else involved and he hadn't been horrible to her. I considered that I might be doing her a favour in demonstrating that it was OK not to keep seeing a man if you'd decided that you'd be happier single; I'd seen the other option happen with friends in the past. They dated, they liked each other, they were nice people, everyone around them was coupled up, and so they'd carry on dating. And maybe they'd decide to move in or even get married because, well, it was time, really; they weren't getting any younger and all that crap.

Then one of them would fall madly in love with someone else, or find something he or she really, really cared about that the other person wasn't into, and there would be an awful, messy break-up or, even worse, they'd decide to stay together, maybe have some "relationship counselling", and spend the rest of their lives boring each other to death. By the end of the night, I thought I'd got my point across well enough. At least when I told Belinda that I wasn't going to be seeing Robbie again she hadn't come out with any crap about betting I wished I'd stayed with Phil. I supposed that at some point it would come out that I'd actually shagged one of the Kings' Men – too many people in the folk world knew one another for it to stay a dark secret. With any luck, though, by the time anyone did make the connection, I'd be able to laugh it off as one of those unfortunate coincidences and no big deal.

I definitely wouldn't be getting back with Phil, though. For all I knew, he'd found someone he was genuinely happy with by now, and I wished him well. I pushed him out of my mind and carried on tossing clothes onto the bed.

I finally unearthed my blue and lilac flowered skirt from the back of the wardrobe. I didn't often wear skirts, let alone flowered ones, but this was brilliant for ceilidh dancing. It was roughly knee-length, but it was cut so that it flared out whenever I did a turn, flashing a lot more leg than you'd expect, and the bright, cartoonish pattern of it always made me smile. I put a plain lilac T-shirt with it, and my electric-blue Doc Martens, and spiked up my hair with a bit of glitter gel – it might be a bit dated, but I still liked doing it. My favourite silver leaf earrings, black eyeliner, neon-pink lipstick, and I was ready to roll. I didn't bother with a handbag, just shoved my wallet, phone, and keys into the pocket of my grey jacket, and went out into the warm spring sunshine that was just starting to fade.

The Spring into Action ceilidhs were always held mid-April, just before what most teams regarded as the start of dancing season. You didn't have to be an actual Morris dancer to go along, though the majority of the people there generally were. It was usually the Middlesex and Hertfordshire teams who turned up mob-handed, as the venue was a community hall on the far side of Uxbridge and a hike for anyone who lived south of Harrow, really.

When I got there, the dancing had already started. The floor was full of six-couple sets doing something heavy on stripping-the-willow. I spotted Mel and Katie halfway down one set, and Leah sitting at a table near the back of the hall, minding coats and pints. I waved to her and indicated that I was going to get a drink for myself, and she waved back.

The hall was a fairly modern building, with one big main room that was excellent for dancing. It had a terrific sprung wooden floor – they hired it out for aerobics classes and kids' street dancing and stuff, or so someone had once told me. Other than that, it was high-ceilinged and airy, with a few smaller rooms along with the usual amenities like loos and a kitchen. It didn't have an actual licensed bar, but they'd made arrangements to have a few barrels of beer set up on a trestle table in one of the side rooms, with a couple of crates underneath filled with bottles of white and rose wine, cans of Coke, and bottles of mineral water. I bought a pint of Doom Bar and made my way back to where I'd seen Leah, just as the dance was ending.

'Rachel's here, and Dawn too,' Leah informed me, reaching out to haul another chair over. 'Jayne said she was coming, but we haven't seen her yet.'

'What about Belinda and Susy? Any sign of them or did they bail out?'

'Bel's otherwise engaged.' Leah rolled her eyes.

'Apparently some mate of hers is having a party with loads of fit single men guaranteed to show up. Susy's got her mother-in-law for the weekend, so she can't make it either.' We'd all heard about Susy's mother-in-law, an allegedly tight-fisted, tight-knickered, and hypercritical Aberdonian, on more than one occasion, so we pulled suitably sympathetic faces. Even Allen, Susy's husband, found his mum a bit tricky to deal with, or so Susy had told us.

People were busy forming up sets for the next dance, and I took my jacket off and looked round the room, wondering what it was going to be and whether to hunt for a male partner or just suggest to Leah that we leave the table unattended and dance together. Katie and Rachel reappeared just then, towing Jayne along with them; she'd just arrived and was raring to go. As Katie confessed herself knackered after doing two dances in a row, Jayne, Leah, Rachel and I hit the floor together, with the usual giggly squabble over who was going to "be the man". It ended up being me and Jayne, with Jayne partnering Leah and me Rachel, and we were soon hurtling back and forth and swinging each other at the corners and having a whale of a time.

One of the things I loved about ceilidh dancing was that it was nigh on impossible to think about anything else when you were doing it; you could just lose yourself in the music and the steps and the figures. Well, as long as the band was good and the caller gauged the audience properly, of course – but that was all in place on that night. I danced with Katie as my partner, then I got asked to dance by a nice old boy who'd once been a member of Holly Bush, a bit before my time with them. I danced with Dawn's husband, Derek, and a friend of his whose name I didn't actually find out, who was a good dancer but smelled a bit sweaty. After about an hour, I was sufficiently shattered to decide I'd sit the next one or two out; I was pouring with sweat and my knees were aching a bit. Mel, who had been dancing every other dance with some bloke in bright red trousers, came and joined me at the table, looking equally ready for a breather.

'Bloody good night, tonight,' she said, grabbing a random pint off the table and downing half of it. 'Sod it, sorry, was that yours?'

'Nah, I've already finished mine. I think we're at the communal-property stage anyway,' I said, looking across the collection of partly consumed drinks on the table. 'Who's your new friend, anyway?'

'Huh? Oh – him. Billy.' Mel grinned. 'I met him at Sidmouth last summer. We didn't ever get as far as swapping numbers, but we just bumped into each other at the bar tonight. He's in Wizard's Hat: you know; that Border side that are actually quite good.'

I nodded, summoning up an admittedly vague memory of a bunch of Border dancers who were a lot better than the usual shambles in rag coats and face paint. There was a history of feuding between male and female Morris teams, but I'd heard some people say it was nothing to the mutual contempt between Cotswold and Border Morris. If you asked a Border dancer about it, you'd get told that Cotswold teams are airy-fairy, posh, and ridiculous, whereas Cotswold dancers would generally say if pushed that Border is for people who can't dance but like dressing up and shouting.

'He looks nice,' I said, more out of politeness than genuine interest. Mel nodded, and drank some more, though this time it was from a different glass.

'He's all right, yeah. Mind you, there are quite a few decent-looking men here tonight. Pity they're mostly Ring members.'

I picked up the nearest drink and took a big gulp of it. I didn't dare look round and scan the crowd. I knew who I would see if I did.

For a moment, I thought about pleading sudden illness and going home, but then I decided that I'd have to get the encounter over with sooner or later, because teams were always running into one another at different events throughout the summer and if it happened tonight, at least I had some mates around me. Surely it wouldn't be anything more complicated than a mutual polite nod and a move away, or at the most a couple of sentences exchanged on the weather, the band, or the beer.

'I need the loo – excuse me,' I said and got to my feet. I could walk round the edges of the dance floor without bumping into anyone or having anyone bump into me, as the dance they were doing at the moment was one of those with lots of standing around unless you were the set's "active" couple. I tried to scan the room without being obvious about it; if I did see him, I really didn't want him to get the impression I was looking for him.

As it was, I made it to the loo – I had genuinely wanted to offload some beer – and back before it happened. I went into the anteroom where the bar was, and just as I made it to the counter, a voice said behind me, 'Can I buy you a drink, love?' I turned around and there he was, and I couldn't actually say anything for a second or two.

He was looking good – of course – in a black vest top and dark olive-green trousers. I tried not to lick my lips, acutely aware of my burning cheeks and probably smudged make-up after all the hard dancing I'd been doing.

'Pint of something? Or are you back on the gin?' His words didn't come off quite as brashly confident as I thought he intended. He was looking at me a bit warily, and it occurred to me that he might actually have been hurt that I'd dumped him via Facebook.

'Doom Bar,' I said. 'But make it a half. Thanks.'

He got the drinks in and handed me mine, still eyeing me as though he thought I might bolt, or throw it at him or something.

'It's that documentary, isn't it?' he said suddenly. 'You know about the Kings' Men, and me. Look, can we talk about it?'

I fought a fast, silent battle with myself: on the one hand I knew I should tell him there was nothing to discuss, thank him for the drink, and scuttle back to Mel and the rest, but I couldn't help hoping he'd have some sort of excuse or justification or reason that would make it OK for me to carry on seeing him. Just then, though, there was a sudden influx of people and I realised the band must have called for an interval. Any minute now, Rachel or Leah or Dawn might come and catch me fraternising with the enemy.

'It's OK,' I said, rather stupidly, because it wasn't OK with me that he was friends or fellow travellers with someone like Alfie Winters. 'I mean, Robbie, I don't want to have a fight with you. And I'm with friends tonight. But I will talk to you later.'

Out of the corner of my eye, I spotted Derek, Dawn's husband, approaching with his friend, clearly having been despatched to get a round of drinks in.

'Oi, will you leave the birds alone and get over here?' someone yelled. Robbie winced, half-turning in the direction of the sound. A small group of men, several pints up by the look of them, had just come in and one of them was beckoning tipsily to Robbie. It clearly wasn't a good time for either of us, so I raised my glass to him and made a rapid exit back to the main hall.

Back at the table with Leah and Katie and the rest, everyone was talking about their aching legs and how hot it was and how good the band were, so I didn't have to put in very much in the way of conversation. The first dance after the interval was a quadrille, and I thought about doing it but then thought I would sit still for a bit while the others danced and try to sort out the mass of conflicting impulses in my mind. It was a bit unfortunate, really, that Robbie had turned up tonight when the whole fancy-the-arse-off-you-but-can't-get-involved-with-you business was still so raw, but at the same time, no matter what we did, we would end up in the same places sooner or later. It was up to me to get over it all and be able to treat him with the same sort of civil, impersonal attitude we all generally applied to members of teams we weren't that friendly with.

He'd asked if we could talk about it, and I had the sinking feeling it would be something along the lines of "can't you just ignore that I hang out with woman-haters, because, well, don't get all feminist about it". I'd sort of expected him to be better than that. I still hoped he might be better than that.

The quadrille finished, and the dancers scattered as usual, with some people hurrying to sit down, some returning briefly to their tables for a quick gulp of a drink, and others pacing the dance floor, waiting to see what came next and how many people they'd need to line up with.

Of course, that was the point the caller announced she wanted a circular set of couples; it was "that time of night", and they were going to do Rozsa. Once or twice in the past, I'd dragged non-folky mates along to ceilidhs, partly to demonstrate to anyone who thought there was nothing sexy about it that they were completely wrong, and Rozsa would be the dance that always convinced them.

I looked round the room again, almost chewing on my lips but refusing to let myself do so. Robbie was standing by the door, also scanning the room, and when we made eye contact, it genuinely gave me a physical jolt. I couldn't explain the effect he had on me, but I strongly suspected it was mutual. He came striding through the crowd, effortlessly avoiding the people who milled around searching for partners, and heading straight for the table where I was sitting, with nearly all the others around me.

'Dance with me?' he said, holding out his hand.

I thought it was pretty bloody brave of him to ask me straight out, in front of my mates and probably a load of his, several of whom on each side were going to know that this was kind of a diplomatic incident, even if they didn't actually know that I was one of the notorious Wenches and he was part of a seriously men-only organisation. At the very least, he risked some serious piss-taking, both from Mel, who was gazing at him with fairly exaggerated shock and had obviously clocked him for a King's Man, and from his own teammates, however many of them saw him. And it would be all the more humiliating for him if I turned him down.

Perhaps I should have, but I didn't want to. I hadn't thought about it at the time, but somewhere in my mind, the night we met, when we danced together at the Harlequin, there had been this little flicker deep down of "I'd like to dance Rozsa with you". The sexiest dance there was; I'd often wanted to have a suitably sexy partner to do it with but it hadn't ever happened.

'OK, yeah, I will,' I said, and we made our way quickly into the ring of couples just as the caller was outlining the steps of the dance for the benefit of those who either didn't know it or had forgotten the sequence. Then the music started, and we were off. And it was probably the most erotic experience I ever had with all my clothes on. There wasn't any actual groping on either side: both of us had better manners than to go in for anything quite as crass as that. Also, obviously, there was the fact that we both knew we shouldn't really be dancing together, and people were going to be looking at us. Somehow, in a nasty sort of way, that made it even dirtier and more intense. I was incredibly aware of his fingertips, of the heat of his body, whether he was behind me, turning me or swinging me, face to face.

I kept wanting to look up into his eyes and forcing myself not to. If I looked him in the eye, I would see the same sort of overriding, consuming desire that I felt, and that might be a little bit more than I could take right now.

Round the circle we both went; slide, sway, turn, forward and back, close and then apart and then close again. Neither of us was putting a foot wrong; not a single stumble or wrong turn. It was just like before, just like I'd known, somehow, that it would be if we ever danced this dance. We were in perfect harmony while the music was playing and I wished it would never stop. My lips were tingling, my heart rate double the time of the band, and I don't think I have ever wanted to kiss someone quite so much.

I'd pretty much tuned the caller out by now, and it probably helped that Rozsa was a simple enough dance that she didn't need to be reminding us all of every figure, but suddenly she yelled, 'One! Last! Time!' and it was almost over. When we slowed to a halt, and the couples around us were breaking apart either with polite thanks for the dance or invitations to come and have a drink, or whatever, Robbie took hold of both my hands.

'Let's have that talk,' he said. 'Come on, let's go outside. I need some air.'

While I knew perfectly well I could have pulled away – and knew, very well indeed, that he wouldn't stop me or make a scene if I did – I had to admit to myself that I wanted to talk it over just as much as he seemed to. Even if the only thing between us was an intense, physical lust, it didn't seem to want to go away.

Another of Mel's sayings came to mind all of a sudden: "If you don't know whether to follow your head or your heart, follow your fanny!"

Chapter Six

We went through the bar, down the corridor and out of the side door, still holding hands. They left this exit open for the sake of smokers, but at that point, it was free of people standing around and trying to wreck their lungs under the one heated wall light above the ashtray, which I was quite glad of.

Robbie led me along the side of the building until we were well into the dark, at the edge of the tangle of trees and bushes that marked the boundary between the community hall and the rugby pitch. I was seriously considering just dragging him in among the trees, pushing him against the nearest sturdy trunk, and ripping all his clothes off when he said, 'I'm really sorry you had to find out like that. I should have just fucking told you.'

I took a step back, remembering the horrible shock of seeing him on film, large as life, standing behind that ignorant, sexist arsehole who'd just insulted my whole team.

'How do you know? How do you know that I know about you?' Because, fine, one of the Kings' Men getting together with a Waterleigh Wench was a problem, but when I'd dumped him, I hadn't actually given him the reason, had I?

'Valerie, of course,' he said. 'We had a session

with them, Thursday night round at this studio in Hammersmith. "We're going to do some interviews with you, nothing tricky, just an informal thing – oh, and we'll show you what we've done so far with all the other teams." And they showed us your lot seeing that bit of film from the Wassailers Day, and that's when I worked it out.'

'What did you do?' I asked. I was shivering, just a little bit, and part of that was down to it actually being quite chilly now we were outside in the dark.

'You're cold, come here,' Robbie said, almost distractedly, and hugged me close to him.

'I didn't do anything. I didn't know what to do. Not then. I looked you up on YouTube when I got home, by the way. You're all really good. It was quite a turn-on, watching you dance.'

Being cuddled against him was warm, and felt lovely. He'd said he was sorry, and I had my arms round him now, my head on his shoulder, and I was breathing in the scent of him and starting to feel even more wobbly at the knees. Suddenly, I didn't want to have a row about his team and my team, and whether or not women could dance. Maybe we should just forget about it, for tonight at least. Maybe it wouldn't do any harm to have one more night with him. No one else needed to know, after all. But then again, was it fair, to either of us?

'I don't know,' I said, thinking out loud. He held me a little bit tighter, and kissed the top of my head.

'I know what I want to do,' he murmured.

'Would it involve a snog?' I said. I lifted up my face and he didn't need another prompt; he just kissed me. We kissed hard, and deep, and long, pretty much using each other so as not to fall over, and I could feel myself melting, opening up, pressing more tightly to him.

We broke apart, eventually, and I looked at Robbie and looked away. I could hear music coming faintly from inside the hall, but couldn't identify the tune. There was just about enough light coming from the building's windows for us to see each other, and probably enough for anyone else who came outside to see the pair of us.

'It's a long way back to Hackney,' I said, before I could overanalyse things any more. 'Why don't you crash at mine? There's a bus goes to Uxbridge Tube station from here.'

He didn't reply for a moment, which made me think he was going to turn me down, and that would have been utterly humiliating, but then he said, 'I'd love to. I'd really love to. Thanks, Cath.' And then he kissed me again.

Of course, we then had to contend with getting ourselves out of there and back to South Waterleigh without having to make it obvious to our respective friends and teammates we were travelling together. Robbie had come up with three other Kings' Men in a car belonging to one of them, but he said that as long as he told one of the three he was making his own way home, they wouldn't make a big deal out of it and nag for details. There were a few more of his team there, but he didn't actually know whether they were getting the Tube or cabbing it to Denham for the last train back into London. As for my side, Dawn and Derek had one of those massive people-carriers, and would be taking two or three of the others back at least as far as Eastcote, but that would mean at least two more Wenches likely to be on the Tube, as well. And there's nothing like a long-ish Tube journey for awkward conversation when you're doing something that's, well, potentially awkward. As Robbie and I strolled back toward the side entrance, I could feel myself blushing at the thought of sitting there with a fixed grin on my face while Mel or Leah or Katie made needling remarks in Robbie's direction and snide ones in mine. Oh sod it, now I was acting like a 15-year-old, and being fairly unfair to my friends, who might take the piss out of me in private but probably wouldn't actually make me look stupid in front of the man I … I didn't actually know how to finish that sentence, so I was glad I'd been saying it in my head rather than aloud.

'There's only about 20 minutes to go,' he said. 'Do you want to make a move? Just so we don't get stuck sitting in a carriage with your mates at one end and mine at the other, like a shit rom-com.'

He was echoing my own thoughts so closely yet again, and it made me snort briefly with laughter. He had his arm round my shoulders still, and gave me a slight squeeze.

'Great,' I said. 'Meet you at the front entrance in about ten, OK?'

Back in the main hall, the only person sitting at our table was Rachel, which was a stroke of luck; out of all of us, she was the most laidback, so I just picked up my jacket and said, 'I'm off now, see you on Tuesday,'

She said, 'Fair enough, night night,' and carried on watching the huge Grand Chain that was in progress on the dance floor.

Robbie was standing just inside the door, reading the various leaflets on the noticeboard, when I caught up with him.

'All sorted?' he asked, reaching for my hand.

'No worries,' I said, and we headed down the long, dark driveway together.

We didn't talk much on the way back to mine. I was glad Robbie didn't take the opportunity to have another try at discussing Our Big Problem, because I didn't want to think about it. The train we caught was nearly empty, as we'd managed to beat the closing-time rush, which at least meant no squealing hen parties or drunks bellowing at one another, and we both fell into that kind of trance state you can get on the Underground, gazing blankly across the carriage at the black walls rushing past the window. I felt tired, but in a good way, my legs not exactly aching but aware of how much I'd danced that night. I was also thinking about dancing with Robbie, and then about that kiss at the edge of the playing field, and anticipating what we were going to do when I got him into my bedroom. I couldn't help grinning to myself, just a little bit.

He reached up and stroked the back of my neck, and I felt my heart rate speeding up.

'Next stop, isn't it?' he said. 'Do we walk from there, or get another bus?'

'We'll walk, it's only about ten minutes,' I said. I had a sudden urge to kiss him again, but just at that moment, the train started slowing and the lights of the platform surged into view.

I had a moment or two of anxiety when we reached

the end of my road, trying to remember if I'd picked yesterday's cast-off clothes from the bedroom floor before I left: crumpled discarded knickers on the carpet don't give the greatest impression. I knew the kitchen was tidy enough, and I've never been the sort to keep things like pile ointment or ladies' moustache bleacher in the bathroom cupboard to freak out snooping visitors. Whatever. It would be fine. It had to be.

Once we were inside my flat, we had one of those moments of looking at one another a little bit warily, a little bit self-conscious.

'Do you want a drink? Coffee, tea? I haven't got any beer or anything,' I said. Robbie half-laughed.

'It's all right, Cath. I don't want anything – well, not a drink, anyway. Or are you having one?'

I shook my head. It suddenly occurred to me that, after all the dancing and the excitement, I could actually do with a shower before bed, and I had a sudden mental image of us showering together, so naturally, I shared it with him.

'Sounds good,' he said. 'I'll wash your back and you can wash … any bit of me you like.' Once again, he was coming out with comments that would have sounded either cheesy or crass from anyone else, and I felt that hot, deep flexing inside my quim again.

'Come on, then,' I said and led him through to the bathroom.

Because my flat's quite small and the bathroom's very small, I only have a shower: no bathtub. But that does mean it's quite a big shower, so there was room for both of us, without any uncomfortable bumping of knees and elbows against the door or soap dish catching anyone in the small of the back.

I got the water running before stripping off, to give the slightly moody boiler time to get going, but it didn't seem very long before we were face to face under the spurting jets, kissing and running our hands over each other's sleekly wet bodies. Robbie had been half-erect when he took his pants off, and it didn't take more than a couple of kisses for his cock to be fully hard, rigid and jutting upwards, pushing against my stomach when I wrapped my arms around him. I wriggled gently to and fro, but I knew I wasn't quite the right height for us to fuck each other standing up. Never mind, there were plenty of other things I could do.

I reached for the bottle of shower gel, hanging on its useful hook, and helped myself to a good dollop of the stuff. It was a citrus-and-something, not so flowery that it would raise eyebrows if the scent of it still clung to Robbie's skin the next day.

'Lean back,' I whispered, gently pushing him against the wall and then licking and softly biting his nipples, which had stiffened almost as much as his cock. I rubbed the shaft of it with the shower gel, working up a little lather so my hand could slide easily up and down the length. He groaned, closing his eyes and bracing himself against the tiles. The water streamed and gently pounded over us as I wanked him, speeding up and slowing down, twisting my wrist a little, pumping up and down that hot, pulsing shaft, tense and straining upwards, the head of it bulbous and free of the foreskin.

'Cath, oh Cath, love, you're so good at it,' Robbie gasped, and I worked him a little faster, leaning over to give his left nipple a firm suck, while I used one hand up and down his prick and the other to cup his balls, cradling them in their vulnerable sac of warm, wrinkled skin, feeling them tighten, listening to his ragged breathing.

'If you don't stop soon … I won't be able to …'

'That's all right, that's fine,' I said, and it was. I wanted to make him come, I wanted him to lose control for me. I knew it wouldn't be long; I looked up at his face, watched him throw his head back and cry out, and then his cock spasmed in my hand and let loose jet after jet of pearly white seed.

'Oh my God. Sorry, love, I just couldn't hold it,' he said, straightening up and pulling me against him. He kissed my temple, then put a finger under my chin and lifted my face so he could kiss my mouth, a quick, firm press of his lips to mine. 'I've been thinking about it for days. Ever since last Friday. And I didn't last two minutes.'

He glanced around for the shower control and switched it off. 'Can we get into the bedroom and I'll do something good for you?'

We towelled off quickly and I led him through to my bed, which was barely big enough for two, but at that point, I really didn't care. I lay down, and he lay beside me, running one finger slowly over my skin, tracing circles round each of my breasts, working his way up to the tightly crinkled peak of each nipple then outwards again. It was gorgeous, but torture as well; so tantalizing I could hardly bear it. I spread my legs, almost involuntarily, my hips beginning to push up and my pussy opening for him. He licked my nipples then, circling them with his tongue the way he had been doing with his fingers, and I dug my nails into the bed beneath me. I was so dripping wet now that I thought I must be dampening the sheet.

Robbie made his slow, steady way down the bed, turning himself carefully until his face was between my thighs. He started to lick me then, his tongue flickering delicately over my clit, his breath hot on my mound. He said nothing more, just licked and licked, holding me open with his hands on my legs, tasting me, scenting me, the tip of his tongue keeping up the intensity of the stimulation. My stomach muscles were quivering, my heart beating so loud I thought the whole of the street could probably hear it, and still he kept on licking, nothing but those dainty little licks, focused entirely on the most sensitive spot. And then I grabbed the back of his head and pulled his face against my cunt and came and came and came.

Once I could see and think straight, and breathe again, Robbie had picked the duvet up from the floor and draped it over us both. It must have been about two in the morning, and it was chilly by then, and both of us were tired. So, after a few minutes of wriggling about, we settled into the classic spoon position. I think he fell asleep before me, because I lay awake for a while, thinking there must be some way things could be sorted out, but knowing that there really wasn't.

I woke up first, at about nine o'clock, and got gently out of bed, managing not to disturb him. I'd never really understood the word "heartsick" before, but that was how I felt. It wasn't just that I would miss him once I'd thrown him out; it was an awareness that bringing him back to my place and doing all those gloriously dirty things we'd done together had been, well, a bit unfair. Because I'd known, and he hadn't, that I was only going to give him the one night – or the second night, to be picky about it.

I tiptoed into the kitchen and poured myself a glass of grapefruit juice. It looked like another sunny spring day outside, which made me feel worse. There was no way I could carry on seeing him, no matter how good we were in bed together, no matter how good we were on a dance floor together, even. It would be like a vegan dating a meat packer. His teammates might laugh and slap him on the back and talk about all women really needing nothing but a good shag, and mine would probably say nothing to my face but feel betrayed, all of them.

It wasn't just that Robbie danced with a Ring side. It wasn't just that letting the documentary crew get even a sniff of a "good human interest story" would end up a completely embarrassing and degrading experience and probably ruin the chance we had to show people what Morris dancing could be about. It was the idea of people thinking I didn't mind about dating someone who hung out with an arsehole like Alfie Winters, that I had so little self-respect I would stay with someone who probably really did think, on some level, that women weren't entirely human.

I started to cry, just a little bit, not making any noise. I was going to have to be polite, and calm, and cheerful: not a tear-stained drama llama. I could do it. Of course I could.

Despite the sunshine, it was too cold to be sitting there starkers, so I went back to the bedroom, got my old grey dressing gown from the back of the door, and put it on. It wasn't a very sexy garment, but I decided to wear it anyway; nothing sexy was going to happen this morning.

Robbie was still sleeping, the duvet half-on, half-off his body as he lay on his side, one arm stretched out as though it was still around my waist. I wished, briefly, that he'd rolled onto his back and gone in for a bit of open-mouthed snoring so he looked a bit less irresistible. I thought about waking him and telling him to get dressed and go, but it seemed a bit brutal; I could at least let him sleep as long as he wanted.

Just as I was forming that thought, Robbie gave a sigh, wriggled a bit, and then rolled over, opening his eyes.

'Hey, love. Morning.'

'Hi,' I said, pulling my dressing gown more tightly round me. Robbie sat up, clearly getting the idea that something was wrong.

'I'll put the kettle on.' I took the traditional get-a-breathing-space option and headed quickly back into the kitchen. He came in a moment or two later, barefoot but otherwise dressed, and sat down at the wobbly little table. I got a couple of mugs from the draining board.

'Tea, coffee, or there's some grapefruit juice,' I said, brightly.

'Coffee's fine. Black, please.'

I made the drinks, listening to myself clattering about and feeling clumsy and silly. I put his coffee in front of him and retreated back against the sink with my own.

'We didn't talk about it properly, did we?' Robbie

said. 'You and me, and the dancing, and the TV crew, and all that shit.'

'There's not really a lot to talk about,' I said, and gulped some coffee, burning my tongue. I banged the mug down on the worktop and forced myself not to start pacing up and down.

'Cath,' Robbie said. 'Cath, love – we need to sort this out.'

'No,' I said, surprising myself a bit. 'I don't think there's much to sort out. Look, we've had some fun but ... you know; the whole rival team business. I think we'd better just leave it at that.'

'Leave it at what? Never talk about Morris when we're in bed? I can live with that.'

For a moment, that seemed desperately tempting – ignore each other in public and screw each other senseless in private – but I quickly got a grip on my yearning libido.

'No, that's not what I meant. We've had a bit of fun, but – well, probably better stop there. It's too ...' I couldn't find the right word. There was a miserable tightness in my chest, and it was hard to say anything. Robbie was sitting very still, almost holding his breath.

'It doesn't – it's not – is it because of Alfie? Because of what that old git said? Is that why you're dumping me?' He sounded horrified.

'It just wouldn't work out,' I said, and I was proud of how steady my voice was. 'It's been nice, but I think it's better to let it go, OK? I expect we'll see each other sometime over the summer. You got any bookings coming up?' It felt easier to switch back to a sort of cheery, sociable mode. 'We've got quite a full calendar, how about your lot?'

'We're doing Waterleigh Bridge Market on the May Bank Holiday,' Robbie said. 'That'll be fun. With the sodding camera crew, as well.' He shoved his chair back from the table, got up and went to retrieve his shoes. I stayed where I was, because I wasn't sure what else to do. He reappeared a moment or two later. He looked about as rough as I felt, his face set and unhappy.

'I don't want to tell you what to do, or what to think,' he said. 'But I'm not your enemy. I'm not like that. You can trust me. I wish you would.' He looked down at the floor, digging at it with the toe of his trainer. 'I wish all this wasn't in the way. We could be really good together. We are. I mean, we were. I'm going to make a twat of myself any minute, so I'll just go home. But I wish you'd think about it. Think about me.'

I wrapped my arms tightly round myself, holding on, staying calm. I was amazed by how much it hurt to see his pain. It was ridiculous, really, for either of us to be this bothered. I wanted to reach out and take his arm and lead him straight back to bed, and kiss him and stroke him and ride him hard until that look of aching sorrow left his eyes. But the problem would still remain, the awareness that we were too different, and in the end, it would poison everything.

I set my teeth and dug my fingernails into my own arms.

'I'm sorry it turned out like this, really, I am,' I said, very quietly. 'Take care of yourself.' I couldn't even summon up the good-hostess manners to walk to the door with him; I just stood where I was, taking slow, deep, determined breaths so that I didn't crack up and howl, or call out to him to say I'd changed my mind, or any other stupid clichéd bad move I could think of. I heard the door close behind him and I picked up my half-full coffee mug and smashed it in the sink.

That made me feel really stupid and childish, so I spent the next couple of hours cleaning, scrubbing, and sorting out the pile of junk mail and bank statements and pay slips, and generally being useful and dutiful. Just as I was running out of chores, I got a text from Joanna, saying that she and Miles and some of their friends were going to have lunch in the Red Lion at Richmond, and I'd be welcome to join them if I wasn't busy. Given the choice between that or sitting at the kitchen table crying all afternoon, it was no contest, so I went and showered again, put on my favourite jeans and a black T-shirt printed with little skulls all over it, and made for the Tube.

At first, it felt like exactly what I needed. Jo – and Miles, to an extent – were good friends, and also pretty much entirely outside the world of Morris. An afternoon with them involved a bit of gossip about the old days when we lived in Shoreditch, a bit more gossip about what everyone else was up to right now, and various drinking stories and silly jokes. We all ate enormous platefuls of roast beef and Yorkshire pudding, and more bottles of wine kept appearing on the table and in the ice bucket, and I was feeling happy and entirely in control, right up to the moment when Joanna said, 'So, that hot man you picked up at the Harlequin the other week, what happened there? Anything good?'

I opened my mouth, but nothing came out. Around

the big table, everyone else was still drinking, discussing whether they were going to have a pudding or not, complaining that they'd eaten too much, but it was as though everything had just skidded to a standstill around me.

'Cath, what's the matter?' Jo said. 'Are you all right?'

I gripped the edge of the table. If I said anything at all, I was going to howl.

'Come to the loo with me. Come on. You daft mare, let's go and you can tell me all about it.' Jo was in command, as she'd always been in our Shoreditch days, and I followed her to the ladies', already sniffling and leaking tears.

Luckily it was a big, roomy set of loos, with a wide sink area between the cubicles, and even had a couple of chairs set on one side of it, so I could sit and have a proper cry, with Jo gathering handfuls of loo roll and passing them to me at intervals. When I'd told her the whole story, I gave my nose a final blow and said, 'I suppose you think I'm just being a twat about it.'

Jo frowned. 'No, you're not. It seems a shame, though. I mean, it's not as though he was the one saying horrible things. So, what do you expect him to do about that other bloke? Shoot him?'

'It's not like that,' I told her, wetly. 'Obviously, they've all got a right to their opinions. But I don't want to go out with someone who doesn't mind or thinks it's no big deal. Alfie Winters is horrible, and if Robbie's friends with him then I don't want to know, do you see?'

'Sort of.' Jo went and got a dollop of hand lotion

out of the dispenser and started rubbing it into her skin. The lemony scent reminded me of showering with Robbie, and I forced the thought away: no more grizzling. There was nothing more to say, really.

Chapter Seven

It was a perfect day for dancing: dry, bright but not too hot for the beginning of May. The Waterleigh Bridge market looked thoroughly inviting when I got there, at about 11.10. I could see a range of stalls selling all sorts of stuff – jewellery, clothes, old records, handmade soaps – and the sun was sparkling on the river that ran along one side of the place. I was going to find a way to enjoy myself today. I was determined about that.

Just over a fortnight had gone by since I'd seen Robbie. He hadn't tried to ring me, or send me any messages via Facebook, Twitter or any other way at all, and I tried not to be annoyed by that. I had dumped him, after all – if he'd made attempts to get in touch I'd have been angry that he wouldn't take no for an answer. No one had teased me at practice about going home with someone from a Ring side, so it was possible that the others either hadn't realised that I'd done more than just agree to dance with him, or reckoned that it was up to me who I might choose to lust after. It might have been the fact that we were really pushing ourselves to get our dances chosen and perfected for the Waterleigh Bridge gig – and the first actual dance-out, on the first of May, as well: we weren't really inclined to talk about anything other than dancing when we were in the Horseshoes.

During the rest of the time, I kept busy with things like going out for a curry with the rest of the IT crew and meeting up with Meg and Jo and Amanda to go and see a film. I was happy, I was contented, I was throwing myself into my life and not thinking about men or sex at all. And I'd laugh at anyone who told me otherwise, I promised myself.

I glanced toward the Stag's Head, a big pub right by the entrance to the market, as that was where we'd agreed to meet. It had a kind of terrace that opened out into the market itself, and I could see Jayne and Dawn, already in kit, standing there with pints in their hands, and Mel tuning her fiddle. I could also see, at the other end of the terrace, a clutch of Morris men, clustered close together and deep in conversation. I swallowed, and quickened my pace. I'd been keen to believe there wouldn't be any direct contact between us and the Kings' Men, except for perhaps a stiff exchange or two about who was going to dance first, but I supposed it was only natural that they'd be in the pub as well. Morris dancers require beer, after all.

The ladies' was echoing with the sound of Morris bells, as Leah, Susy, Belinda and Katie were all in there, sorting themselves into their kit and doing their make-up. They were chatting about the May Day tour we'd done, and the pub that had given us free beer, and how many people had wanted to know if we'd been dancing at dawn that day. I said hi to them all, slid into a vacant cubicle, and quickly put my own kit on; the blouse, the waist-cincher, the little skirt, and then my bells. I came out again so I could use the mirror to get my headscarf properly tied, and found there was a bit more space as both Bel and Susy had gone to the bar.

'All right?' Leah asked, while I was doing my lipstick.

'Fine,' I said, hoping I sounded like I meant it.

'You seemed a bit low on May Day. Is everything all right?'

I winced. I thought I'd been doing so well. But then again, Leah was the sort of person who noticed everything and didn't miss a trick.

'It's fine,' I said again, though this time my voice wobbled a bit. Katie finished tying her own headscarf and came over to give my arm a squeeze.

'You know where we all are if you want to talk,' she said.

'In the meantime, tits and teeth,' Leah said, and then I did manage a smile.

We went out onto the terrace for a headcount and a pre-performance huddle. Katie asked Dawn if she'd sorted out the order of dancing with the Kings' Men yet, and Leah added something about having to deal with "that fat old git; how was he?"

Dawn grinned.

'Not here, apparently. Some rather nice young man came over and said he was acting Squire today, and would we like to toss a coin for who goes first. I said it was fine if they wanted to start, and they're on in a couple of minutes.'

'Which means we'd better be ready,' Mel said, and then, 'Oh hang on, here comes Happy Valerie.'

We all glanced round and saw Val, striding across the expanse of courtyard that was obviously the designated dancing spot. With her was a pretty, Goth-looking woman with long, fair hair, who appeared simultaneously amused and put out.

'Everything OK?' Dawn called out. 'Hi, Lucy, thanks for having us.'

The Goth blonde grinned.

'Glad you could make it. You and those boys; it should be a good day. With no aggravations, all right?' This sentence was to Val, and I wondered what the undercurrents were in that department, as there clearly were a few.

Val, once she'd reached us, obligingly made her position clear.

'I was explaining to Lucy that it would be fun if we made something more out of the rivalry between the two teams,' she said. 'Maybe getting the crowd to vote on who they prefer, and seeing how that works for all of you.' She smiled at us all, and it occurred to me that she had very big, very white teeth. Predator's teeth. She didn't care about us; she wanted to see a good fight.

I had a sudden ghastly vision of us being barracked and booed offstage by the Kings' Men and their supporters, with Robbie at the front of it, getting his revenge, and the whole stupid mess being broadcast to the nation. I swallowed hard and banished the mental pictures: he couldn't be that idiotic, could he? And then I started getting annoyed with myself for being so unfair to him, even if it was only a paranoid fantasy.

'And I was explaining to you,' Lucy said, with equally firm cheerfulness, 'that this is an enjoyable family day out, not Battle of the Morris Dancers. So we'll have no booing or throwing things or trying to start a fight, OK?' She looked round at the assembled Wenches.

'I'm really looking forward to seeing you dance,' she said. 'And the pub's laying on beer and snacks for you all at two o'clock, when you've finished. I'll just go and make sure the other lot know that, as well.'

She headed off to the other side of the terrace, where the Kings' Men were just lining up, clearly about to embark on their first dance. Val glanced from Mel to Dawn and took a deep breath. 'I hardly think anyone would start throwing things,' she said. 'But a little conflict, especially when it's actually there ... It would make the programme more ... relevant. Not that you're not relevant, of course.'

None of us spoke, and Val was smart enough to let it lie.

'I'll leave you to get on with the dancing, then,' she said, only slightly sulkily. 'We're just going to film the dancing, unless anything else happens. Well, we've made a start already. Anyway ... Dance well, everyone.'

'We always do,' Mel said. 'Whatever those Ring-dings might reckon.'

At that point there was a burst of music, instantly recognisable as *Lilibulero*, which got a few of us sniggering and crossing our fingers: if there's one tune you can rely on to start a fight, it's that one. We headed to the edge of the terrace in a very loose formation, leaving Rachel's husband, Gerry, and a mate of Leah's who'd come along to watch, in charge of our kitbags and general junk. I was at the back, which no one had objected to, and as we drew closer to where the men were dancing, I straightened my spine and took a deep breath. I wasn't going to give anyone a flicker of an indication as to how I felt. Not one flicker. I wasn't sure if I felt better or worse for the news that Awful Alfie wasn't around. It would be ridiculously paranoid to think that Robbie might have told the man about me, and what had happened – somehow I couldn't quite believe there was that much of a friendship between them – so Alfie Winters would have no reason to single me out for any more unpleasantness than he was generally inclined to dish out to women dancers.

Of course, it then occurred to me that Robbie himself might have decided not to show up. He might have thought it was the gentlemanly thing to do, to avoid any more awkwardness or embarrassment for either of us. I winced; somehow, I didn't like that idea very much. I didn't want to think I'd spoilt the dancing season for him to the extent that he'd have to avoid any event the Wenches might be appearing at.

I'd been staring hard at the back of Katie's head, but now I forced myself to look up and take in what the Kings' Men were actually doing. They weren't all old wrecks, as they'd previously been; there were about 15 of them, there but only a single set of six up for this dance. They'd mixed younger and older dancers, but the older ones were clearly the fittest of the veterans, because they all looked well matched in the figures.

Robbie was dancing second corner and I kept myself hidden behind Katie so I could watch him properly.

Oh bloody hell; he was worth watching. Unlike some Morris men, he didn't look remotely daft in his sash and ribboned hat, and he moved with the same natural grace and confidence I'd fallen for the first time I saw him on the dance floor at the Harlequin. I couldn't help it; a huge appreciative grin spread over my face, then melted away as I remembered that I'd dumped him, and he was unlikely to have anything to say to me.

Susy, who was next to me, dug me swiftly in the ribs as they finished the dance and walked off in a slick, professional line.

'That blond one's a bit of all right,' she whispered. 'Even if he is a King's Man.'

I struggled to keep my face – and my voice – reasonably neutral.

'Yeah. Know what you mean.'

'Hang on!' Susy wasn't slow on the uptake. 'Isn't that the one you were dancing with at the ceilidh? Holy shit, Cath –' But at that minute Dawn told us all to move on out, and there wasn't time to say anything else.

As all eight of us were out today, we were going to start with Mixed Double, a dance we'd evolved last year, which we liked to use as an introduction to a performance. It needed a lot of concentration whether you were in the outer or the inner circle of it, and I was thankful for the need to keep my mind on my movements. I definitely didn't want to fuck up or trip over in front of the Kings' Men, and wouldn't have under any circumstances. Mel played three long single notes on her violin, and off we went: in and out and round, two sidesteps and a jump and through the centre, and then the same thing again … We finished with a flourish and then the inside four made a small set and the outer four, which included me, filed off and got out of the way, to quite a reasonable level of applause.

The Kings' Men had taken up a spot at the other end of the dancing space, by the stall selling soaps and bath stuff. I sneaked a look in their direction, half-expecting them to have all turned their backs on us, but to my surprise, at least half of them were clapping, and it didn't look particularly sarcastic. I spotted one of Val's cameramen, as well, zooming in on the Kings' Men and then turning to focus on Katie, Leah, Rachel and Bel as they went through the next dance. Robbie had been one of the ones applauding, but he wasn't looking my way.

For the next couple of hours or so, we danced in turn, and I made myself concentrate entirely on that, whether I was up in a set or standing back with those who weren't. There was very little communication between the two teams, other than a word or a nod from Diane or the shaven-headed, broad-shouldered one who appeared to be in charge of the Kings' Men in Alfie Winters' absence. It didn't feel too bad. As long as I kept silently repeating that statement to myself, it was almost true – at least as long as I didn't look in any direction where I might expect to see Robbie.

When our spot was over, Val joined us in the mass migration toward the pub. It was clear she hadn't got what she wanted out of the day; even her hair was bristling with irritation. She didn't say anything, at least not to us, but I noticed her collaring the bigger of her cameramen and having what looked like a very intense conversation with him.

The Stag's Head had set aside the small bar for us, and there were jugs of beer and trays of food set out, but the Kings' Men colonised one side and we, led by Dawn and Mel, occupied the other. We all took our bells off, and removed our headscarves, but everyone was too hungry and thirsty to run off and change: besides, while we were still wearing most of our kit, we still looked very much like a team, I thought. I poured myself a pint and put some sandwiches on a plate, and sat at the table nearest the window where Susy and Katie were in a position that screened me a little from view, or at least from the view of anyone else in the bar.

I picked up one of my sandwiches, and took a bite: ham, cheese, and coleslaw, and all of it fresh and delicious. The bread was seriously crusty too, which meant that when Susy said, 'So what about that bloke, then, Cath?' I could take temporary refuge in chewing. Just as I reached a point where I would have to either engage in a conversation with her or take another big bite in a way that would probably make it obvious I was refusing to talk, Valerie clapped her hands.

'We're just going to film a little bit in here, while you're winding down,' she said, loudly. 'So just go on with your lunch and don't mind us.'

'Wouldn't you rather get a bit of drama, Val?' said one of the older Kings' Men, a chunky character with an ostentatious moustache. 'We could tell you why we've sacked our Squire. On camera. Sorry we didn't actually wait until you were around to do it, and all that.'

Valerie did a kind of goldfish face at him, which was almost certainly copied by everyone at the

Waterleigh Wenches tables. I didn't realise how hard I'd squeezed the sandwich I was holding until I put it down on the plate and realised my fingers were slick with mayonnaise.

'You sacked your Squire,' Valerie murmured, wonderingly. Then she turned fast toward the cameraman and snapped, 'Get this, now!' He scuttled up behind her, shoving his camera, mic attached, almost up the nose of the man who'd been speaking, and Val said, 'So, you've made some changes in your team?'

'Had to be done.' It wasn't Moustache who was talking, though. It was a voice I knew very, very well. I'd been trying so hard not to even look in the Kings' Men's direction but now I knew that every one of my team was staring over at their table as Robbie waved a friendly hand at the camera. He didn't look at me, or at us: just straight down the lens.

'There's a limit to how much crap anyone'll put up with,' he said. 'Alfie went way beyond it. We weren't prepared to put up with any more.'

He did look in our direction then, and Valerie said, 'So what was the last straw? What changed your minds, as a team?'

Robbie pushed himself backwards, hands on the table. 'We'd just had enough of his attitude,' he said. 'You want a soundbite? Tradition's fine, misogyny's for losers.'

He delivered the line with the same swagger I'd been so turned on by over the past few weeks: he knew it was cheesy and he knew it was right and he was going to say it and see what happened.

'Hallelujah!' Mel shouted, and I let out a little

squeal of pure surprise; I had actually forgotten that the rest of my team were sitting there and listening.

'Oh, you *have* got a keeper there,' Susy said in my ear. 'I'd say go and give him a kiss, but Val would like that waaaay too much.'

'I don't know what you mean,' I retorted, a bit desperately, just as Valerie brought the cameraman over to the Wenches' side of the bar.

I didn't take in what she said, or what Mel or Dawn or Belinda had to say in response. I was too busy staring, stupidly, across the room at Robbie. He was talking intently to one of his teammates, but then he looked up, looked at me, and raised his eyebrows.

I grinned. I couldn't stop myself.

Luckily, Mel and Dawn had enough to say on the whole business to stop Valerie getting the cameraman to turn his attention to me for more than a general shot of a few of us looking pleased. The Kings' Men, out of shot, were busily appreciating the food and drink, and I kept my head down as much as I could, until the documentary crew retreated, and Katie and Rachel started making noises about heading for home.

'I'm going to have a look round the market,' Dawn said. 'I haven't been here for ages.'

'Me too,' Belinda said, and she and Leah went off to the ladies' to change.

I sat where I was, and finished my drink, carefully avoiding any glances in the direction of the Kings' Men table. I was vaguely aware that most of them, like most of the Wenches, were sorting themselves out to go their separate ways, and I was happy to wait where I was for a little while longer. Eventually, still not looking at the other side of the bar, I went and changed into the jeans and team T-shirt I'd arrived in, dawdling over the procedure, my senses jumping and my pulse racing.

When I came back into the bar, Robbie was the only person there. 'Hey, Cath,' he said.

I stopped in my tracks and allowed myself to look at him properly. He was leaning against the door that led back into the pub, still in his white shirt, but without his hat or ribbons.

'We kicked him out,' he said. 'You're right. He's an arsehole. But I'm not.'

I couldn't say anything. I could barely breathe.

'I'm not,' Robbie repeated. 'Would you let me prove it? Or try to prove it?'

It took me less than two double-steps would have done to cross the distance between us and take him in my arms.

Epilogue

They showed the documentary on one of the satellite channels over the August Bank Holiday weekend, at ten o'clock on the Saturday night. Val did email Dawn at the end of June, as soon as the date was set, to tell her this, and Dawn passed the news on to all of us at practice, provoking a chorus of derisive laughter from most of the Wenches and only a small wail of protest from Belinda. We would all be spending that particular weekend under canvas, joining in with the Merry Maidens' annual Summer's Farewell, a small but brilliant festival we'd been invited to. So anyone who wanted to see *Thoroughly Modern Morris*, as Val and co had titled their effort, would have to rely on TiVo or iPlayer or whatever they had, when they got home again.

A couple of the Merry Maidens, being old pals of Dawn's, did say the clubhouse bar at the campsite would probably be happy to let anyone who wanted watch the thing on their TV, but that idea came to nothing in the end, and we were all so fully occupied with enjoying the festival that it all but slipped our minds. It certainly wasn't something I was thinking about, but then the Summer's Farewell was kind of my first public weekend with Robbie, as both our teams were dancing at the event.

Our teammates on both sides knew we were seeing each other, of course, and if anyone had a problem with it, then they were keeping it to themselves. I was pretty sure none of my friends thought I was a collaborator or that I'd betrayed us, or any old rubbish like that. Susy had dragged me off into a corner at the first practice after May Day to ask what had happened. I'd told her, a bit hesitantly, that I'd gone home with him that night and she'd just squealed with glee and told me to get stuck in. Mel had sat herself next to me in the pub that night and said that anyone who could dance like "that long-legged blondie of yours" was bound to be all right, and there had been a fair few cheerful little comments about diplomatic relations the first time I went to the Three Kings pub to meet Robbie after he'd been to practice. We were doing fine, we both reckoned, and we'd talked before the weekend about the fact that people generally weren't as concerned with anyone else's affairs as much as with their own. Still, when I was packing to set off for Summer's Farewell, I'd kept thinking about the way most people in the rest of the Morris world knew that there were issues between the King's Men and the Waterleigh Wenches. I'd been pretty prepared for long looks and muttered remarks.

As it turned out, the dancers who were there who knew the King's Men were more interested in the fact that Alfie Winters had left. Robbie said he almost lost count of the people who sidled up to him to say well done and about time, too. There were rumours going round that Alfie had retired from Morris altogether, or that he was setting up a new side of his own, or that he had joined the Garrick Morris Men, a team who were supposed to be so rabidly anti-women that even the Morris Ring had their doubts about letting them join. To be honest, I couldn't say I cared very much. I was revelling in the whole business of being at a festival with Robbie. We were dancing with our own teams at different spots during the bulk of the days, but in the evenings we were watching the bands or dancing at the ceilidhs or just sitting on the grass with various friends, counting the stars and holding hands. It was the most idyllic weekend I'd had since I started Morris dancing, and I wasn't going to spoil it by fretting about a stupid TV show.

Robbie and I ended up watching a recording of the programme in bed together, at his place, on the evening of the Bank Holiday Monday. We'd decided to share his tent for the weekend as it was bigger than mine, and also that I'd stay over when we got back, as it was easier to get to his place than mine. Summer's Farewell was held near Milton Keynes, so car-free types like him and me would be coming back into Euston and I could just brave the Piccadilly Line to get to work in the morning, rather than dragging myself all the way back home with all my gear on the Monday night. Of course, that did mean leaving some of my stuff at his place until Friday, but we were both OK with that.

We'd basically fallen into this entirely comfortable relationship, ever since Waterleigh Bridge: nights at my place, nights at his, hanging out with friends, hanging out together ... I'd never been so happy in the whole of my life. Whatever might happen in the future, I was going to enjoy what we had for as long as possible.

We got in at about eight o'clock, tired and grubby, but still feeling pretty good. It had been a hot, sunny weekend so at least we weren't lugging wet tents and bedding but, as usual at the smaller festivals, there hadn't been much in the way of shower facilities. Robbie said that if I let him have first go in the bathroom he'd go out and get us something to eat while I was taking my turn, which sounded fine to me. I went and made myself a cup of tea and checked my emails, Facebook and Twitter, which were all jumping, just a little bit, with comments from people who'd already seen the documentary. I deliberately didn't read any of them.

Robbie went off to forage for food, as he put it, and I had a good, wallowing bath and then put on a little something I'd been hiding in the side pocket of my rucksack all weekend. It was a set of transparent mesh knickers that tied at the side, with a matching floaty babydoll thing to wear on top. It was brilliantly tacky and blatantly sexy at the same time, and I knew he'd appreciate both sides of it. I'd bought it on eBay a few weeks previously and decided, when I was packing for the festival, to sneak it into my bag and wait for an appropriate moment.

When Robbie came back in, I was lying on the sofa with my hands behind my head and my legs crossed in a look-at-me-I'm-a-sex-goddess way, and he dropped the shopping bags on the floor.

'Oh God, shall we just have a fuck right now and supper later?' he said. 'Or do you want feeding first?'

I had intended to go for the deferred gratification option again and tell him we should eat, and watch the documentary, and then maybe have a bit of fun. Sometimes savouring the anticipation really worked for both of us – but then again, I'd slipped a condom under the sofa cushions, just in case, before getting into position. It was just as well I'd done that, because the look of naked, absolute, unashamed lust on his face went straight to my groin, and I felt myself opening up, getting really wet.

'Get your pants off and get over here!' I said, and my voice was choked with need.

He kicked off his trainers and walked toward me, pulling off his T-shirt and undoing his shorts on the way. I pulled the ribbons on the knickers, unfastening them and displaying my juicy sex. Robbie fell on his knees by the sofa and started to lick and suck my nipples through the fine mesh of the babydoll. I found the condom and passed it to him, and started stroking myself while he put it on. My clit was throbbing, pulsing, and my pussy was aching for him.

It wasn't going to be possible to do it on the sofa so I pushed him down onto his back on the carpet and lowered myself onto him, taking him deep inside me, holding him down and riding him. Robbie pushed up into me, reaching for my tits again, caressing and squeezing them while I rocked back and forth on his cock, clenching my cunt muscles, telling him how good it felt, and then he pulled me down to kiss me hard and deep, and we were both coming, almost at the same time, coming good and hard, lots more kisses, pressed tight together, laughing a little at how quick it had been, holding each other tight.

He'd bought some Prosecco as well as various bits and pieces of finger foods but, being Morris dancers, we drank the fizz out of our tankards while we watched the show. It really wasn't bad at all. As well as the Waterleigh Wenches and the King's Men, there was stuff about a mixed Cotswold side who were nearly all the offspring of previous members, and a Border team who were massively into the alleged pagan aspects of the whole business. The last lot did come over as a bit twatty, but they weren't treated unsympathetically. Dawn and Mel appeared, talking about the reasons they'd set up the Wenches; Mel in particular went into detail about some of the other "weird" Morris teams that had inspired her, like the White Rats from the US, and Prince Albert Morris in England.

'Kinky Morris?' Robbie said as he scooped chilli jam onto a cracker topped with Brie. 'I wouldn't mind getting them to come out with us some time.'

'What, dancing or just for a party?' I was going to carry on but then the programme cut to the footage of Alfie Winters spouting his anti-women crap. I tensed myself against the rush of outrage and humiliation I expected to feel, but seeing and hearing him again didn't bother me nearly as much as it had done the first time. Robbie was more upset than I was.

'I can't believe we put up with him as long as we did,' he said. 'He was always a dick to new dancers, as well.'

I gave him a gentle pat on the thigh.

'He's gone, babe, you won't even have to think about him again. Ooh look, there's us!'

On the screen, the Wenches were dancing *Country Garden*, and Dawn's voice on the soundtrack was explaining the way in which women kept the dances alive and that Morris was for everyone and anyone who wanted to do it. Then there was footage of the King's Men dancing, and even I thought it was a little bit unfair to focus so much on the older members and their occasional missteps. However, the next bit was another montage of about 30 different teams with visibly younger dancers and various not-entirely-traditional costumes, with a voice that sounded like Val's saying, 'Morris in the 21st century has many faces, and the old-guard position of not taking women seriously looks to be on the way out.'

And here was Robbie, filling the frame, explaining how Alfie had been chucked out of the team.

The real, live Robbie in bed next to me gave a yelp and hid his face on my shoulder, but I was watching with a deep, thrilling sense of satisfaction. I kissed the top of his head and said, 'You done good, babe.'

A few more beeps came from the sitting room, where we'd both left our phones, and I suspected that quite a lot of our teammates had been watching recordings of the show around the same time as we had. Still, I wasn't about to go digging for their opinions for the moment. *Thoroughly Modern Morris* was drawing to a close with another montage of mostly female teams, now, so I put the tray of snacks on the bedside table and wriggled myself into a nearly horizontal position. I was feeling sleepy, and happy with it.

'Going to be talked about,' Robbie said as the credits rolled. 'Well, not quite *Britain's Got Talent* standard, but people are going to talk.'

'Doesn't bother me,' I said. 'It'll all blow over in a week or two.'

Robbie used the remote to kill the TV and lay down himself, pulling me into his arms again.

'We won't, though, will we, Cath?' he said. 'We'll stick around, stick together.' Once again, I heard something softer, more vulnerable behind the words, and I wrapped myself around him, holding on tight.

'We will, babe, we will.' And then I giggled to myself as the words popped into my head and I knew I could say them and he'd get what I meant.

'A hard dancer is good to find.'

Other titles that may Xcite you

For more of our titles please visit our website

www.xcitebooks.com

Printed in Great Britain
by Amazon

34492867R00067